ESTᴰ 2009

№8

{REWRITING MASCULINITY}

EDITOR-IN-CHIEF	the drevlow
EDITORS	kassie bohannon
	darren winters
	jonathan baker
	andrew harvey
COVER ART & DESIGN	ryan w. bradley
ADVIDSORY BOARD	jared yates sexton
	christopher wolford
FOUNDER	jarrett haley

Dedicated to examining the evolution of modern masculinity from the voices that most often get drowned out amongst the shouting and posturing—voices that often struggle in silence.

Whoever you are, whatever you identify as, and wherever you come from, we want to hear from you.

If you're hurting, if you've got things you need to let go of, things you need to let out, if you don't quite know how you fit into all this we've been told we should fit into, if you think you're the only one, we're here for you.

№8

ISBN 13: 978-1-7985769-9-1

table of contents

ANIMALS

nicholas rhys

When I was young, my old man told me we were all animals. He told me this often as I sat on our green carpeted floor and thought about the pig rooting around in the mud and the grizzly pawing at the tree and lions from the zoo with their awful roar.

For a few years after the mills first shut down, my old man worked as a C.O. in a prison the next town over. Day in and day out he put up with shit from over a thousand inmates. Day in and day out he heard people shout out things like "Fuck you, you fat piece of shit!" and smiled and broke up their fights and watched them eat and lift weights and play basketball.

The other guards wondered how he did it—how he didn't break every once in a while, didn't crack an inmate over the head with his baton or yell insults back at them like they all did. They invited him to barbeques and gave him a plaque and clapped him on the back when he arrived in the mornings and left at night.

But when my old man came home from work, it was different. He would eviscerate my mother when our dinner was from the frozen food aisle. He would snarl at me for having no discipline when I didn't have my homework done, or tear through us both because he had had a long day and just wanted to drink a beer or two and have a warm, homemade dinner with his family.

Sometimes he hit us, would sigh and say he hated to do it, but we left him no choice.

I remember one night when our phone rang at three in the morning waking me up. It rang for what felt like infinity before someone answered it. The next day my old man looked at me and, for the hundredth time, said, "Adam, you know we're just animals. All of us. You and your mother, too."

I had had enough. I yelled at him. I told him it wasn't true. I told him we were different—we were better than animals, and he laughed. My old man laughed in my face and said what makes you so sure?

I didn't know that that late-night phone call was from an inmate who escaped from the prison where he worked. I didn't know the guy used to harass my old man every day for three years—said things to him like, "I'm gonna get you, you mother fucker. I'm gonna get you when I get out of this fuck hole."

I didn't know the man had murdered his wife and two children, didn't know why my old man had our address removed from the phone book the next day, didn't know why he started going to the shooting range, and I didn't know why he and my mother fought about that instead of overcooked meat or frozen chicken patties at the dinner table.

During gym class a few weeks later, Brian O'Donnell stood in the corner the entire period while we played basketball. He stood there and growled at everyone the whole period. Even Mr. Ryan rolled his eyes and left him alone. Everyone laughed at him, laughed right in his face. But I didn't. I walked up to Brian and he looked right at me and kept growling, and I looked back at him and told him he was right.

THE LAST HOURS OF A HORNET

frank reardon

The blood settled on the old English letters of Alan's knuckle tattoo that spelled out the word *Nana*. Forty-three years of failing at everything knocked him on his ass. Tears filled up his eyes and dropped down on his cheeks. He wanted to wipe them away because when he was a young boy he was taught *Men don't cry*.

The sickness in his gut was getting to be too much. It felt like a swarm of hornets. He needed a fix but his friend, Joe, who had been letting him stay at his house the last few years, was kicking him out. Alan had become too unpredictable. His emotions were up one moment, the next calm, the next depressed.

Alan had been snorting a crushed-up Vicodin to help with the dope sickness when Joe knocked on his door. Joe had given him two weeks to find a place to go, but Alan was too concerned with trying to work his day job at a gas station and finding his fix in between to even bother looking for a place to go. Alan knew he had exhausted all possible couches, rooms, flea bag motels, and homes of family members over the years to even bother. The idea of living on the streets in the middle of winter scared him enough to pretend it wasn't happening. If he ignored the situation long enough, it would fix itself. Joe would forgive him and let him stay. The harder Joe knocked, the louder Alan turned up his music.

Joe and his wife, Darla, had been easy on Alan over the years. They grew up together. They traveled to Dead concerts together, and later on, Phish concerts. It was during this time that Alan picked up an interest in China White from a woman named Alex from Pittsburgh. Alex and Alan developed a relationship. He truly loved her, and he thought she loved him, too, until the summer concerts were over, and she returned to Pittsburgh, leaving Alan with a broken heart and a full-blown addiction.

Twenty years went by and Joe and Darla had gotten married and had a few kids. They settled down in an old house they rebuilt themselves in Reading, Massachusetts. They ran into Alan at a concert in Boston one night. Alan was coming down from his high but having the time of his life. Moving to the music. Feeling the energy of the crowd. He didn't care that he was forty years old. Joe and Darla decided to take him in. Joe, a recovering alcoholic, knew a few things about addiction and wanted to help. Darla, a mother to everyone in her long, flowing, handmade hippie skirts, hugged Alan until they got home that night. Alan never said a word. He never cried.

The police had to be called several times a year once Alan moved in. He was erratic at best. Even though he lived up to his promise of finding a job and keeping it, he scared Joe's kids. They'd find him smacked out in the living room in front of Discovery Channel shows about lions in Africa. He didn't talk right. Moved in slow motion while the world around him was in normal speed. It was Darla, who after a couple of years of trying to help, made Joe kick him out. She couldn't face doing it herself. She truly loved Alan and stayed up many of nights with him just talking about life, the universe, music. The love she showed him over the years is why Alan spared her the beating he had just given Joe moments before.

"What did you do, Alan?" she said. Alan didn't respond. She watched him clench and unclench his blood-soaked fists. Years of being nobody to no one pumped through his veins like ghosts unable to find their tombs.

Darla turned the corner of the staircase and looked through Alan's open bedroom door. She could see the band posters on the wall. Alan lived like he'd been stuck in his early twenties. She treated him like he was her helpless son, an orphan she had found at a concert, a child whose own mother abandoned him a long time ago; he was more than happy to live that way.

"Joe?" she kept saying, until she made it almost to the top of the stairs and found Joe lying on the ground. Joe's face was a bloody and messy pulp. His eyes were swollen shut. She noticed two holes in the wall and a laundry basket of spilled clothes around Joe's feet. Blood dripping from Joe's face had formed a tiny pool in the fibers of the off-white carpet.

She moved backwards down the stairs. Alan looked up at her then looked back down. "I'm taking the kids and leaving now," she said with a tremble.

"You're going to let us go, right?" Alan's head shot up. He wanted to ask her if she'd take him with her, too.

He wanted her to take him by the hand and run him across the snow in search of help. The both of them could find a home with a light on, where an elderly couple would let them inside so Darla could call the police and tell them her and her son, Alan, were attacked in their home by depraved bandits demanding money. Alan wanted the elderly couple to sit down on either side of him and console him, to look up from their embrace and see Darla on the phone worried about him from a distance.

Darla went into her bedroom and grabbed her two kids watching television on her bed and went out the backdoor in search for help. Alan reached into the pocket of his jeans and pulled out three Vicodin pills, popped them into his mouth, and chewed. He locked the deadbolt to the front door and went to the sink to wash his hands.

Under the running water his knuckles were raw, ripped and swollen. He stared at the *Nana* tattoo on one hand, and the *Pops* tattoo on the other. They were two people that loved him unconditionally when others wouldn't. His own mother stopped talking to him the day she found him dope sick in her house. His father, who divorced his mother when Alan was a baby, was never seen again. His mom remarried a few more times, but the marriages always ended. Alan never really understood why he had numerous step fathers in and out of his life. They were not bad men. They didn't beat him. They tried to care for him. They tried to fill a space that was vacant, but his mom, a happy light that reeled in men and created marriages and a life of promise, always turned into a silent darkness that wouldn't leave the bed until divorce papers were signed.

The three Vicodins eased his mind enough for him to figure out a plan. He went up the stairs to check on Joe. He couldn't believe what he had done. All his friend wanted was a happy family without a junkie under his roof. It hit Alan that Joe had tried longer than anyone else, years longer, but Alan snapped anyhow. He opened the door mid-knock and went to work on Joe's face with everything he had, and once Joe was on the ground, Alan straddled his chest and landed a dozen punches more. A punch for Alex who got him hooked. A punch for a father who abandoned him. A punch for a mother who had failed him. A punch for a brother who stopped talking to him. A punch for a sister who went down the same path his mother did. The rest of the punches were out of disgust for who he was, for what he'd become.

Alan leaned his ear near Joe's mouth to check for breathing. The nerves pumping through his body prevented him from hearing anything. He placed the palm of his hand on Joe's chest to see if it was moving, but his hands were too numb from the pills to get an idea. He fell back on his ass and put his back up against the wall and lit a USA Gold menthol cigarette. He ripped the Grateful Dead ball cap from his balding head and threw it on the ground. To the right at the end of the hall was a long mirror mounted to a closet door that people used to get ready in the morning. He'd seen Joe standing in it a million times before fixing his hair. He'd make fun of Joe until Joe laughed and left for his job as a school bus mechanic for the city.

He'd watched Darla putting on makeup in the mirror every morning. She'd turn her head full of blonde hair around and ask him, "Do I look good, honey?" He'd always tell her yes so he could get that motherly hug before she left for her secretary job at the local gas and heating company.

Now all he saw in the mirror was a skeleton of a man. Straws of black and thinning hair. His face was narrow. He looked like he hadn't eaten in a decade. A person could run a pencil across his ribs and create music to dance to. His waist was a size thirty, not good for a man who was nearly six feet tall.

Darla had tried to get him to eat but he was always too high, looking to get high, or trying to kick. The times he did try to kick, Darla stayed up with him all night, rubbed his back as he got sick over the toilet, hugged him when he imagined things that were not there. She sat with him in N.A. meetings. She encouraged him to talk about his past when all he wanted to do was run to the far corners of his mind from it.

One time he was successful. He put on nearly twenty pounds after two months of being sober. He thought about going to trade school to become an HVAC technician. Joe even drove him to the local community college to get the application. They all went out for beers and dinner together. It started to seem like old times. Darla even introduced him to one of her work friends, Jen. Alan dated Jen for a few months, but when it wasn't working out because Alan was broke and didn't have his shit straight enough for her, she left him. Not long after, the feeling of being alone set into his bones, and he started using again.

Alan jumped up from the floor when he heard Joe force out some air. He leaned in and shook Joe's body. Joe spit out some blood from his lips but still didn't move. Fear pumped through Alan's body when he heard loud knocking on the door. Relieved that Joe was alive, Alan stood up and walked slowly down the staircase. The knocking got louder.

"Reading Police Department!" a voice from behind the door yelled.

Alan said nothing. He walked towards the door but changed his mind and started to walk backwards. He looked out the back window and saw the long backyard filled with old cars, lawn mowers, and bikes that Joe had worked on. Snow covered the wheels, and bike handle bars popped out from their white graves in search of an owner to save them. Beyond the yard Alan could see into the woods. The dark February sky held onto the moon like a jewel in the center of a ring. It gave off enough light to expose a path.

"Reading Police Department!" the voice yelled again.

Alan opened the backdoor and went outside without a jacket. A sweatshirt frayed around the neck from years of use and the old Dead ball cap were all he had to protect himself from the cold fifteen-degree winter night. He made it to the path and walked far enough in and stood behind a moss-covered boulder. The police had entered the house by popping open the door with a crowbar. A few minutes later, he could see enough into the windows to watch Joe being carried on a stretcher by the EMTs. Alan thought about walking in with his hands up and surrendering, but the flashlights being carried by the officers in the backyard changed his mind. He ran deeper into the woods.

He kept running through the cold without a plan. The pills started to leave his body. When the hornets returned to sting his insides he wanted to vomit. He kept running. *Maybe prison will get me straight,* he thought in between puffs of cold air exiting his lungs. *Maybe this is what I need?* He collapsed in the snow to catch his breath. He rubbed his arms to try and rid his bones of the frigid temps. Far off he heard police sirens up and down Main Street. He knew they were looking for him. He looked at *Nana* and *Pops* tattooed on his knuckles, then cupped his hand and blew air into them to try and warm them up.

He realized where he was when he could see the dark roof of the gas station he worked at in the valley. Main Street Gas was more than seventy years old and the building looked like it, too, tilted to the side with a wooden fence that wrapped around the back of the building. Inside the fence, dozens of old rusted-out cars sat silent in their mud-holes since the 1970s or earlier. The cars were without seats and wheels. Some without hoods, engines, and doors; they comforted him. He got the job from the original owner's grandson, Craig Swanson. Craig didn't put money into the place; in fact, if it wasn't for Craig's promise to his grandfather, he would've sold the land a long time ago to developers.

Alan used his Pops' name to get the job. When he was a kid it was the only place Pops would get gas. The ride to the station in Pops' Cadillac was a high point in his youth. Old Reggie Swanson would be sitting his fat body in a chair in front of the station, sipping on RC Colas until someone came for gas. Pops would talk to Reggie for twenty minutes about nothing. They'd look at cars his son was working on in the garage. Pops would drop a quarter into Alan's hand for a glass bottle cola from the ice chest. It might've been the early eighties, but Old Reggie made sure the place stayed 1950s. Reggie would be damned if his life's work became a Golden Arches.

Craig gave Alan the same job as Old Reggie. Regardless of his age, Alan loved having Reggie's job of sitting in front of the gas station on warm summer days, waiting to fill up cars heading for destinations unknown. Alan did his work with a smile. He'd talk to anyone willing to talk. He had friends come by and talk to him about what had been going on in their lives. But what Alan really wanted was for Pops' Cadillac to pull up. He wanted to see the tall man many said he resembled get out of the car and drop a quarter into his hand. Alan wanted Pops to confess everything to him. Tell him about Germany and World War II. Tell him about his struggles with alcohol and morphine after being sent home with bullet wounds to his leg and ribs. He wanted Pops to tell him how he overcame alcohol and morphine for his family of six, how he remained positive in the physical fight of his life. Pops had died several years before, and Alan knew it, but somewhere inside he never gave up hope of seeing Pops pull into the station to greet him.

The station closed early, a rule from Old Reggie's days. He'd always say, "If you need gas in this town after six, then you ought to go to one of them fancy new Chevron Stations that sell frozen pizza. I'm in the gas and auto repair business, not the breakfast sandwich business." Alan worked there from seven in the morning until six at night for minimum wage. The last auto mechanic they had quit seven years earlier. An old Taurus was still in the garage, abandoned years before by its owner who didn't want to pay for it. Alan tried to fix it but couldn't. He had never been good with tools.

Alan had one of two keys to the place. Craig Swanson owned the other key, and Craig only came by once a day to collect the cash in the safe and to pay Alan out of pocket.

Alan made his way through the snow and woods, stopping behind a tree anytime a cop cruiser flew by, or slowed down to shine a light into the woods. He climbed the back fence and landed on the hood of an old Plymouth. He looked at it as the sickness took over his body. Once it had been sky-blue and carried a family to Little League games where fathers and mothers ate hot dogs and cheered on their son's game winning hit. Now it was dead in its spot for thirty years or more, no longer carrying anyone anywhere, forever trapped on its piece of land. Never to be moved again, until God's Wrath, or even worse, a land developer, plowed through it. He made his way through the graveyard of rusty cars until he reached the backdoor of the station and unlocked it. The heat wasn't on, but it was a huge improvement to being outside.

He collapsed in an old leather chair that squeaked when it swiveled. The chair had once been Old Reggie's chair. Nothing in the place had changed in years. The office was surrounded by big filthy windows, and there was an old desk with order forms from ten to fifteen years ago. Alan never got rid of any of them. It gave the place some class, he thought, something all the other stations were missing. An old rack behind him had some cans of oil, a few cans of fix-a-flat, and other things someone could buy for under five bucks to fix their cars.

The lights remained off and he sat in the center of all the darkness. From the street a person wouldn't notice him. He slowed his breathing and crossed his hands over his stomach and waited on no one. He had no plan, no idea of what to do, and even though he was scared of what would become of him, he felt an easy feeling of the past slip into his drug-sick body.

The olive-green phone on the desk worked. He thought about calling someone, but who would he call? He had used up all of his phone calls over the last twenty years. There was no one left to call. He wasn't even sure if anyone would want to take his call. For a second, he fooled himself into thinking his mom would want to hear from him, but he hadn't spoken to her in a few years. She lived less than fifteen miles away and knew where he lived and what he did with his life, but she didn't want to hear from him. Same with his brother. He'd given up on Alan over a decade ago. Dom was the pride of the family because he hustled, made money, and gave money to conservative politicians. Dom married a beautiful woman. He had a son Alan couldn't visit. Even though Dom was the result of a short-lived marriage to a much older Italian man, Alan's mom preferred Dom over him.

He thought about calling his sister, Candice, who was once like him but got over her demons. She had four daughters from four different fathers, one daughter she wasn't even sure who the father was, but it didn't matter to Alan's mother, because Candice overcame her troubled past. She had a job as a Wal-Mart manger. She had a silver badge that said, "Ten Years of Service." Her blue smock was decorated with tiny silver and gold pins for achievements in selling store discounts and for persuading customers to go to the local blood drive. Candice's kids worked in beauty salons or went to community college. They went from bastards to beauties of the ball in the eyes of Alan's mother.

He felt truly alone, away from everything and everyone. He wondered why love had forgotten him? Sure, he was a junkie. He had troubles, but up until beating Joe senseless, he'd never hurt anyone. He only loved people, even if the love came from a place of decaying flowers and darkening flesh. He wasn't put on the earth to wallow in the sadness of it. He lit up a room no matter where he went back-in-the-day. Then somewhere along the line he became everyone's problem they wanted to forget, like cars in the back lot, whispering words that were heard but couldn't be understood.

There was no one to call. He wanted to tell someone a secret. He wanted to say words of peace to anyone who'd listen. He wanted to rip the beating beauty of his heart out of his chest, slam it on the table, and scream out to anyone who would listen: "Please look at me!" "I am here!" "I'm alive!" "I matter!"

The internal want and scream swallowed itself and vanished somewhere deep inside of his body, a place he kept silent for so long that no one could ever find it, including himself. He'd spent years mastering the art of turning sadness into joy, even if it was fake. Though his words to anyone who'd listen were true, he conned himself into believing in the same feelings. He never saw a problem with it. If it could make someone else feel better than he felt, then it was okay to lie to himself.

A dozen police cruisers pulled into the station and Alan watched the lights mix with the dark woods that surrounded the back and sides of the station. He didn't want to run anymore. Twenty years was long enough. He watched several cops get out of their cars then run around and take position behind the cars with their hands bracing themselves around the grips of their Glocks. A tall, fat cop stood in front of the cars. He looked inside and saw Alan sitting in the chair. Alan made no movements. He only returned the same stare the Fat Cop was giving him.

"Alan McDonald," the Fat Cop said. "Come on, boy, time to get up on out here."

He didn't want to move. *How did the world come to this?* he asked himself. *Why does everything have to be this way? Why didn't they love me?*

"I'm giving you to the count of ten," the Fat Cop said. "If you ain't out here, we're coming in. You won't like it if I have to come in there."

Alan saw more cop cars pulling into the station. Some more cops took shooting positions. Others got on their radios. At the end of the lot a TV news vans arrived. He looked on the ground and saw a crowbar underneath the desk. He leaned under and picked it up. He could hear the loud counting coming from the cop's mouth: "One... two... three..."

Alan stood up with the crowbar in his hand. *If I can't be loved in this life, maybe I'll be loved in another one,* he thought. He was tired of the darkness living in his body and mind. He was tired of the pain he caused everyone else. He couldn't take people hanging up on him when he called. He was tired of women leaving him days after meeting him. He was tired of the want to use heroin. He no longer wanted to be one of the relics rotting and forgotten behind the station.

He'd seen all the love he needed to see. He'd heard all the music he was going to hear. He couldn't come back from what he'd done, he knew that with each step fear turned into innocence.

"Eight... nine..."

He opened the front door. The police didn't move from their stance. Onlookers from the street swarmed to the scene like the hornets that had been stinging Alan's stomach. He didn't recognize any of them. The Fat Cop stopped his counting and reached behind his belt and removed the cuffs. Before he could say another word, Alan raised the crowbar and ran towards the Fat Cop's skull. The cops behind the cars unloaded several bullets into Alan's skinny frame. His lifeless body collapsed onto the asphalt. The crowbar hit the ground and rattled somewhere hidden inside the gun smoke. The horror from the screaming crowd silenced his last gasp of air.

HOLIDAY: A MONOLOGUE ON FAMILY & THE THINGS THEY LEAVE BEHIND

adam van winkle

I was born on a Thanksgiving, that old holiday of rape. Works well I guess since he raped Mom on Valentine's Day nine months before.

He felt entitled I suppose and she seemed to accept that as an excuse since it was Valentine's.

She'd done what she thought was honorable and accepted the proposal her daddy and his daddy forced him to make on account a what he done. Don't know what the grandpas threatened him with, but whatever it was it wasn't enough to make him stick around long afterwards.

Mom was not only knocked-up. She was jilted. Me too I suppose. I was causing lots of trouble before I was ever born.

To top it off I decided to come on out on Thanksgiving Day itself. The Marshall County Hospital baby delivery doctor was apparently rather upset he had to miss the Cowboys-Cardinals game.

Here I am, thirty odd years on, Mom gone, still causing trouble. Only this time, I mean to.

I guess I've come to decide that Mom was the kind tried to cause no trouble and wound up bearing the worst of it at times. Better I think to be the one making trouble than getting buried beneath it.

Maybe old Dad came to that same conclusion too a long time ago. That's why he did the things he done. That's why he did the things he done. Cause trouble, run from trouble, so long as you take the proactive approach. Don't just sit and let trouble happen to you. And in a place like this, it most definitely will come one way or the other no matter how meek you might just sit there existing.

Ma sat here and existed for forty-eight years before her heart didn't want to take it no more. It let a valve go and she died in her chair in the living room in the middle of the trailer.

And really I don't have a problem with going out that way myself. It's the living in the mean time I gotta deal with.

Holidays like this. Now.

I mean, mostly this time of year stirs feelings of anxiety and loneliness in me. Of Mom treating dry turkey breast like it was a special meal and me just preferring to have some Spaghetti-O's or Vienna Sausage or both mixed together.

I don't want to just sit around and feel that, the way Mom musta sat around on Thanksgiving looking at me remembering being abandoned before I was born and raped on another holiday. Lord knows what kind of troubled mind she had to sit there with on Valentine's Day itself.

Whatever Mom dealt with the grandpas did their best with me. Taught me to fish and shoot and hunt and stuff. Answered my questions and gave me advice when I had to work on the old ratty truck one of the grandpas give me in high school. That was Mom's dad.

I could tell in some way that Dad's daddy'd been a hell-raiser and trouble-maker in his day, like his son, but something had changed. Maybe he done something he regretted or maybe Dad's mom just cooled him out. Maybe he made the same exact trouble his son done later on to Mom but he was just able to stick it out and deal with it the way he wanted his son to do.

I figure him having trouble in his past whatever it might've been, was why he felt so obligated to me. I was his son's trouble but since his son was his and I was his son's, he felt the need to watch after the chain of trouble he made.

Still got an old truck of course, just a different one than Grandpa's truck. That one blew up beyond fixing some years ago or I'd still have it. I'm sentimental like that.

The knife I use to start my current truck on account the ignition is busted is a knife my grandpa who didn't give the old truck gave me. Apparently, it was my daddy's pocket knife and it got left behind when he took off. It's my knife now I guess.

This truck come off a guy round my age a couple of years ago. It was his daddy's who'd passed. The son drove it some then let it sit some then decided on selling it. I don't think he needed the money, had a habit to support or nothing, just wanted it gone and wasn't too attached. The truck was from the year I was born. I took it as a good sign and give the selling price.

Had it maybe two weeks before the ignition broke, but besides that and regular tune-up stuff the old pickup has given me no trouble.

It has a busted seam in the middle of the bench seat. I just folded an old Indian blanket of Mom's, one she used in that chair quite a bit, and laid her across the seat. Cushion's good and the blanket pattern goes well with the blue vinyl on the seat back. Seems to have stemmed the tearing of the seam.

As I sit under the wheel now, Dad's knife hanging in the ignition, it idles quiet and feels cozy. Homey. More'n the trailer or the porch hanging off the back of it facing the patch of oak trees and poison ivy.

That's where I usually sit to fire my gun. Drink beers and stir up birds and squirrels I see running around in the oak and ivy. Don't ever try to kill 'em, just shoot under, around, above 'em. Scare 'em into doing something interesting for my amusement.

I suppose that's what I'm here to do with Dad. Just shoot around him. Under him. Above him. Near him. Scare him some. For my pleasure.

I bet up to now, he thinks the year I was born was his worst holiday season. That's what made him up and leave his home. Turn his young life upside down. Or maybe he never thinks on it. Man like that. Leaves behind a perfectly good pocket knife and wife and baby boy.

Turns out he never run far. Well not really. He'd been all over working on a seismographing crew. Blowing up dynamite in holes in the ground so some engineers could read the vibrations and check for water and gas and oil and shit. Company he worked for was out of Tishomingo and he'd been renting shitty little apartments around, though spent a lot of nights in motels all over the place on the road crew. Blowing up earth and shit during the day. Drinking in bars and trying to catch skanky women at night. I bet.

When the grandpas died I got all their tackle and rods and guns and knives and shit. So I had my options for this here.

Once my mom's dad's nosy sister who's hell bent on living forever told me she had an old friend that'd spotted my daddy working with that crew a few towns over on a holiday shopping trip, well I guess I started thinking about causing him trouble right off.

Wasn't hard to ask around a little after that, figure the company number.

Call and get his schedule this holiday season.

Told the lady answering phones I was trying to catch up with my dad for the holidays, surprise him on the road. She said he didn't never mention a son but of course that don't mean he didn't have one she figured and it all sounded reasonable sweet to her so she give me the motel address he was at. Even give me the room number.

I figured on one of Dad's dad's guns. That seemed most appropriate. That grandpa was always so guilty round me. He might of shot ol' Dad himself with one of his guns given the chance. But he was dead now like my other grandpa and like Mom. Just had to decide which gun.

Figured a pistol was best since I'd be in the truck cab here, and then figured hell why not my bird and squirrel porch pistol. It's a neat little five-shot revolver still packs a wallop. And it's Dad's dad's. And Dad's like a bird, just flying around, dropping his mess, and flying on. Good choice I suppose.

He's got a second floor room. It's a little two-story balcony motel. Gives me plenty of time to time him and get my mark as he comes outta that room. Locks his door, comes across the balcony, down those big concrete stairs, and over to his shitty little car in the lot.

Man with a job like that and no truck. Just a rusty-mufflered Honda beater. Don't get me wrong. I don't drive no new Beamer obviously, but my old pickup runs good. I bet Dad don't even maintenance his. Bet his don't run near as good as mine. Shame.

Once I got that mark, and once he's halfway across the lot in this autumn early dark, all showered up after work, or not, thinking he's on his way to the bar and another drink and maybe some askance woman to lay later, then I'll make trouble. Then I'll take my shots. Just like on the back porch. Just like when I shoot at birds and squirrels off that old porch I'm gonna make him dance a scared and frenzied dance. Gonna make him panic without even knowing why he's panicked. Just under some primal fear for his life shit. Shots coming from where he cannot know. His next move he cannot plan. Only know that he must move. And fast.

Maybe he'll get so scared and move so fast his heart will blow like Mom's only he won't go so peaceful in a chair. He'll go alone and knowing it in a shitty motel parking lot on the side of the road in southern Oklahoma. But I can't figure that far. That's not how you make trouble.

No to make trouble good you just fire away, what happens be damned. Then you walk away. Or drive away. Like I will. Tonight.

Dad taught me that much. And, this holiday on which I was born, and, every so often, when my birthday's on a Thursday like this one, lines up with my newly given year, I'd like to give thanks to Dad for that. Show him what he passed on to me by running away. Grandpa and Grandpa and Mom may be gone but there's still family in this world.

For that I sit here, pistol loaded, thankful, eager to show Dad my thanks.

MONKEYTAIL AND A GOD

michael agugom

A forest that abhors baskets should not grow mushrooms.
    —Igbo Proverb

My god is lying in a cheap coffin and I'm fighting the urge not to feed him a stick of cigarette.

We're gathered here, in our country-home, to lay him to rest. We are the sheep: Mother, Osi, Chi, and I; we're in the living-room, where he is on display like a new bronze sculpture. We're standing before him, seeing him the last time; or, better yet, he is seeing us the last time. His face, it wears a solemn look; his eyes, shut like when you say The Grace. His palms, on each other, are splayed—those ghostly men and women at Homecoming Mortuary must have kept them splayed. I wonder why they didn't beat his lips into a straight line as well; after all, they claim not to recognise any boundary between the living and the dead: when we went to fetch him, they insisted we knocked before entering the cold-room so that we didn't stumble on the dead frolicking. Well, perhaps, even in death, my god still has a say on his remains. He may have told them to keep him that way. His lips. They are still in the pike shape as when he draws in his smoke. If he begged me for it now I'd give it to him: one last farewell stick of cigarette.

I'm beating down the urge not to laugh out at this picture in my head, of him just lying here and between his lips, a burning stick of cigarette.

Like a painting. I can see him looming before us, majestic, just as in the way he'd hold a stick of cigarette in-between his thumb and index fingers— holding it with grace—to the way he'd wrap his lips around its butt, draw in smoke, and expel grey clouds from his mouth and nostrils. He couldn't do without his smoke. He couldn't even use the toilet without his smoke. He said it helped him pass out body-waste easily. I don't know if he meant it as fact or joke, but it filled me with awe watching him smoke. Every time I watched him, I wanted to grow so fast, to hold a stick of cigarette.

When you love a god, you don't want to be yourself, you want to be him, you stare in the mirror and see him and not you—his voice becomes your voice, his hands, yours; especially when you are just a boy, everything his actions dictate is infallible; you may not even stop to ask yourself if fear and love are identical twins, especially the fear of not measuring up to his standards, fear of failing him, of losing his grace—fear of not being able to even properly hold between your lips a stick of cigarette.

I practised for a while. I would scratch a match, allow the fire to die, quickly bury the match-head in my mouth, and then allow the trapped-flame drizzle out through my mouth and nostrils. Apprenticeship. I became bold. I wanted a real trial so as to graduate quickly and show off: I wanted to prove that blood smells; after all, my god is my father and I am his son and we are one.

Opportunity made me croon. He called me in and sent me to go and buy him a pack of smokes, one afternoon. I was two days behind my eighth birthday that afternoon. I dashed off and sprinted back with it. He picked one out and lit it. He savoured it; I salivated over it. I allowed him finish two sticks. He went to take his bath, and chance beckoned on me to take out two sticks. From the pack. I did and went under the staircase and lit one. A glorious thing: holding that stick between my fingers, just as he does, and lighting it up. But I was surprised when I drew in and choked and coughed. Then, real quick, I adjusted and relaxed to relish that stick.

Either the cough or the spiral flame gave me away.

Father stood before me—imagine how Goliath could have stared down at David; only I wasn't David, I was mini-Goliath. I didn't see this Goliath as threat: I was certain he'd be proud of my attempt to eagerly develop into a Goliath. Dream away.

First, the horror on his face slapped grin off my face, but not the cigarette between my lips. Second, he pulled me out from under the staircase and smacked my face so hard the cigarette flew from my lips. What do you think you're doing?! he bawled. You have the audacity to—he gave me another slap. He dragged me into the house and fetched his leather-belt... The stretch of scar on my body from his belt, it reminds me of an aerial-shot of River Nile

I had seen once on TV. I was in shock the rest of the day.

Hours later, we had a sit-down. That's what wise fathers do after scarring their sons, isn't it? In my head, I momentarily argued for and against the slur of seeing him as a clown.

He began to talk. He said many things. I could hear him as I watched his tar-lips dance, but I couldn't make out the head and tail of his words. *It's wrong you smoked*—this I heard. *My conscience is flogging me*—this I heard. *It's my fault*—this too I heard and asked myself, If it was his fault that I want to emulate him, why did he hit me? What he didn't conclude with was *I'm sorry*; I reckoned it is beneath him to apologise—gods don't apologise. He concluded with a promise to quit smoking. Clown.

He didn't quit; I was glad he didn't quit: I couldn't imagine him without a stick of cigarette, I couldn't imagine our home without the reek of cigarette and the smoke and the ashes and the ash trays—in fact, rather than quit he complemented cigarette with monkeytail.

We file out of the living-room; Mother brings up the rear.

Outside, some feet away from the dug-out grave in the compound, the village women are personae. They are tearing off their dresses, throwing their hands in the air, and tossing themselves on the ground, here and there. They pestle our ears and make our eyes wet with their orgy of grief. All for a god they seem to love and know better than we, his immediate family—or, they want to show us how to grief. Their wails and tear-drenched eyes carry the weight of credibility for the blind. It's normal. Even as their eyes are soggy with tears and grief, they in a few moment later wouldn't be blinded by grief to not scrap over food when plates of jollof rice and chunks of meat, the size of my fist, are passed round. I thought grief steals appetite from the bereaved. They're accustomed to celebrating others' grief, I fear.

My ears catch her before my eyes does: Mrs. Know-all: My God's Sister: Aunty Nnene—she's a bad tooth.

I'm not blind-o to see that he's death is unnatural! I hear her wail. Her voice is head-taller, towering above the rest of the women's. Her words are coarse like my god's palms, bruising my conscience. I can't say if it's doing the same to Mother, too. Mrs. Know-all. She is still singing this accusatory song, a song I pray no one hums to much less nod to. She is bent on changing the tone of this funeral. She's not blind, my foot.

The young men, on the other hand, are statues.

They're solemn beside the heap of brown earth, freshly dug out. Their naked broad chests and tout glistening muscles, would have stood them out as better actors if they had the mind to pull off a theatre like the women. But they choose to be simply grave-diggers. The mid-morning sun is pouring her heat like the rueful stares of the septuagenarians seated under the canopies— I'll get to the root of this, Mrs Know-all shrieks and throws herself on the ground. For attention, I think. Some women try to help her up but she shrugs off their hands. She picks herself up again, I'll be back! I'll confirm the truth. She dashes out of the compound to heaven knows where. She's to Mother and me a naked fuse.

As a boy I saw how Father loved to use his voice and hands.

That night, over dinner, an argument ensued between them: Father and Mother. He tossed big bad words at her; in the same measure, she heaved them back at him. He grabbed her neck and pinned her to the wall with one hand, her legs thrashing in the air. He looked like one monster in Pinky and The Brain. I ran under the bed and watched. Chi, my younger sister, was in a cradle then, crying from her cradle. Father raised his other hand to strike Mother. I joined my voice with Chi's and our cries became shrieks. And he brought down his hands.

The following morning Mother wrote a note.

She packed her things, left the note on the table, and left. Father came in, read the note, and bawled, She's run off! Left me with an infant and a tot! What manner of wife does that! He took Chi and I with him to his mechanic field. After watching him for a while use those same hands dexterously to couple engine parts into whole, I was inspired. I sort rocks as my imaginary engine parts, to couple them into one. While at it, I fell and broke my head. And bled. Perhaps Mother heard of my injury: she returned home later that night and cried and promised she'd never leave Chi and me again. She kept her word but lost her voice henceforth—she became a footnote.

Years later, Monkeytail inspired Father's voice.

Monkeytail became popular, or I grew up and became aware of it: a poor local concoction of hemp roots soaked in spirits. Cheap liquor for broken men. Cheap liquor that offers happy illusions at the price of a damaged liver. Father would return home reeking of it and cigarette. Chi had grown up and Osi was already born too. They were already old enough to wash their underwear clean; old enough for Father to see that he owed us exemplary model. But Father had already grown too old to relinquish this habit, too old to start learning to use his left hand. He would return home at night staggering and crooning: Monkeytail push me go right, Monkeytail push me go left; anything I say no be my fault, na Monkeytail give me voice!

One midnight, Father returned and shook the walls of our home.

That midnight, he's voice was thunder; his eyes, lightning. That midnight, his coarse palm slapped us awake. That night, he commanded us to go and fetch water from the well two streets away. That midnight he ordered us to fill up the water-drum in the corridor, even though we had running tap in the kitchen. That midnight, we, including Mother, obeyed—wobbling between wakefulness and sleep—because that's what god's children do. That midnight, we filled the drum, but Father wasn't pleased yet. That midnight, he ordered us to remain awake with him because he was still awake. That midnight, when Mother tried to plead with him, he barked: Stupid-woman! I brought you from the village to the city! I provide food for you and the children, don't I?! I deserve respect in this house. I'm the god in this house! I made this home!

I had also begun to see Father's fine logic:

When you bring a rustic girl from the village and refine her in the ways of the city and feed her and clothe her and shelter her and provide for the children she bears you, then you have right over her life—even her breathing is at your mercy. Fine logic. But the only reason I had a bitter taste in my mouth as to that logic was that Adaugo my future wife was born in the city and would have been way refined by the time I asked for her hand in marriage. That meant I'd have to shout and beat her more, if not to death, into accepting that I'm the god in our house; hence, for me, tragic logic.

That midnight, to make sure we were really awake, his voice hit the walls and quivered the floor of the room as he turned to us (Osi, Chi, and me) and yelled, Who's the man of this house?

You, Father! was our response.

I say who's the man of this house?

You, Father!
Who's the provider in this house?!
You, Father!
Who's the god in this house?!
You, Father!

The young men now have him on their shoulders, to his grave. We lumber behind. A woman raises a dirge about man coming from the earth and returning to the earth. Mother sings along.

At the mouth of the grave, they lower him in gently. The priest begins to shower him with praises and prayers. Now and then he sprinkles holy-water on the coffin. I can see my god bathed clean by heavenly bodies. His sins, if there be any, are washed away; he's ready to cross the golden gate. He was a good man, the priest keeps saying, as though to remind us in case we had forgotten; and I rationalise that Father was a god who took on the sinful garment of mortals and made himself a husband and father. So he can be excused for any wrong doing while in that garment, I suppose. Perhaps... yes, the reminder of his saintly life by the priest is not merely for our ears alone, but for the invisible angels present to bear in mind. Clown. The women begin another dirge. I sing along.

Singing stops. The Priest gestures at us to step closer to the grave. We do.

Mother scoops brown-earth and throws it in and mumbles, sobbing. My turn: I scoop and throw in a handful and mumble, rest in peace. I can only hope Father heeds to my advice—or, is it prayer, especially now that I am looking down at him, not looking up to him. I don't know what obtains on the other side of the fence; if it is no different from our world here then I doubt he would fare differently there: gods are restless beings. All the same, I wish him rest. Really, I do.

We return to our seats under the canopy marked, Family.

There, is Mother's sister: Aunty Anwuli. The young men are covering the grave. The women have drawn the curtain on their theatre. Then the blanket of solemnity enveloping the compound is sliced open: It's poison-o! she blares. She's back: Mrs Know-all. All heads turn to her as she trots into the compound. My brother's murderer won't get away! She makes a dash for Mother but some women intercept and hold her back. They try to calm her.

She bawls, You know it, Chiamaka! You know about his poisoning. Don't sit there looking innocent. She wags a finger at Mother, The culprit is in this family!

Mother is unruffled. Unfazed. Unresponsive. I don't understand how she can remain so. Then Aunty Anwuli rises in Mother's defence, Let her mourn her late husband in peace, you crazy woman—

The husband she killed!

Mad dog! I can see that dogs have eaten the bag of your mind! How dare you—

You haven't seen a mad dog yet—

Both women continue to scald each other with more burning words and other women are divided into almost equal halves in their support. Accusations and vindications alongside spittle flying over our heads like missiles. My god's funeral turns into a rumpus. I keep my eyes on Mother, my heart thumping. As she draws us out of the chaos, leading us inside the house, her black scarf slides off her neck, fluttering to the ground. And I see the scar on her neck. I remember how and when she got it.

Adaugo said more than her gut should be allowed, in St. John's Hall, when we were playing, after catechism class. She is the prettiest girl on our street and even in Church. I nurse a dream of us getting married when we grow up, so I picked on her a lot. That day, she fired back at me for picking on her, saying, the offspring of a python is bound to be long.

I wasn't irritated at her aphorism, I was irritated by the fact that she still had a voice. Rage goaded me to act: I wanted her to be voiceless like Mother, at once—and all I thought too, in justification, for acting was to be like Father; to, at least, enjoy whatever pleasure he got from it that made him do it always. I grabbed and slapped her good on the right cheek and on the left with the back of my palm. She fell over. I went down on her and held her by the throat and yelled repeatedly, You stupid woman you'll make me kill you one day! Adaugo was choking; I didn't even realise it: I was relishing the thought of doing a perfect re-enactment of what Father did to Mother the night before. It felt amazing until church members gathered and shoved me off of her. Adaugo didn't get the scar as Mother did, but, at least, I made an imitation of Father, an imitation very strong.

Later that night, Father returned home and was quick on the ball.

I wasn't worried. I felt good thinking this was normal manly behaviour for Father to have kept at it. I didn't expect any commendation; I didn't expect rebuke either. He summoned me in and started with his voice: So you went to church to hit a girl? You go out to make troubles for me ehn! Why don't you pick on your fellow boys! Stupid boy...! He yelled so loud the veins and muscles on his neck jut out like pillars. When he finished with his hands, I had a swollen eye and a swelling on my right temple the size of a tennis ball.

The following morning, I stood in front of the mirror and stared hard for me; I didn't see Father in it, never again: I found a bit of me, and began henceforth to look for the rest of me.

Inside the room. My eyes are combing Mother's face for her eyes. She avoids my eyes. She avoids my eyes for her own reasons; I'm looking for her eyes for my own reasons: I want to find her thoughts; I want to weigh her thoughts. I eventually find her eyes, in them I see a frozen heart, a woman turned into a nightmare villain.

Three nights before Father died, Mother sent Osi and Chi to Aunty Anwuli's. I was supposed to go with them but I refused: Mother had never sent us to anyone's home before; I found it strange; strangeness causes me nightmares; nightmares make me bed-wet; bed-wetting in another family's bed is something I could never forgive myself of.

Father returned home tipsy. Mother was happy. Strangely happy. She spoke calmly and petted him. She helped him take his shoes and clothes off. And in gratitude, Father said, Stupid woman, coming to your senses abi? You've finally learnt how to treat a man proper. He spread his hands on the backrest of the sofa to emphasise his lordship. She grinned. She heated water for him to have his bath and set the table and served him dinner.

Father ate his dinner without complaint. Mother waited on him without complaint. She looked blissful in a way I had never seen her; under the lamp-light her face shone. He looked content. I retired into my room and dozed off, happy that for one night our home enjoyed the peace of a graveyard.

The crash of a fallen cup woke me; Mother's voice drew me out of bed. She was kneeling, hunched over Father while he writhed on the floor groaning, Chi-a-maka ple-ase, clutching his tummy and throwing up. She was cooing to him, Now where's your power ehn! Are you no longer god! Get up and hit me... She was lost in her rage, oblivious of my presence behind her at the bedroom door. I stood there frozen to the spot, for a moment the scene looked unreal: How did this god fall, at the mercy of his own creation? Abruptly, he stopped moving. She stopped talking and spat on him. And I saw her shoulders relax as though a heavy load had been lifted off her. And the reality of it all shook me to blurt out, Mother! She turned sharply to me in shock and cried, Nna, Oh myGod! Nna, I'm sorry!

It is three days now and there is mad rapping on the door. The sweet taste of yam porridge in my mouth has turned sour. Mother goes to get the door. I put my spoon down and try not to cuss. Instinct tells me my god has risen to torment us.

At the door are Aunty Nnene and a policeman. Policeman mutters to Mother; Aunty Nnene glowers at Mother. Mother steps out of the way, the due amble in. Mother disappears to change into a gown and reappears. She ties her scarf and say, Nna, clear out the table. I'm going out—

I stand up and ask, What's going on?

I'm going to the station, Mother says.

I'm coming with you, I say.

Mother says, No, you're not—

The Officer, says, yes he is.

Mother freezes and throws the officer a questioning glance.

The D.P.O specifically asked to bring him along, he grins.

Behind the head of the constable at the counter is a placard that says: *The Police Is Your Friend.* I wonder how friendly. Would they be friendly to Mother if the true cause of my god's death becomes as conspicuous as their weakness for bribery?

Mother is coming out of the D.P.O's office, I'm asked to go in now. Her eyes find mine as I pass her. In her eyes I see it: her vindication is in my hands, in my pocket. And I suffer tightness and bitterness in my gullet.

The DPO's moromoro head is so shiny I imagine he polished it with Kiwi Polish, colour-black. His grin, fake; he's throwing it at me generously; I wish

I could just turn back.

I know it's been a difficult few days for you and your family, he begins, but this is also... He seems unsure which road to take to reach me, and then he finds a tunnel. We're in a precarious situation here... I hope you understand what that means... we can't do much from here... what your Aunty brings us is from a source we can't use in a court of law...and we can't dig up your father's remains. I believe you love your father so much to want justice for his death, regardless of who may be involved. It's the right thing to think... So, I just need you to give me truthful answers to the questions... He finally comes around to asking me what I saw the night my god fell, and I look him straight in the eye and say: Father came home tipsy that night; he drinks Monkeytail—two men have died on our street in the past couple of weeks bloated all over from Monkeytail! Monkeytail eats up their livers!

That's all?

Except you want me to lie, sir.

He sighs and falls back in his chair in defeat.

In catechism class, we were taught that truth will set you free. But what truth is the truth that could turn you into an orphan; does sleeping in a government orphanage without the reek of cigarette and Monkeytail count as freedom.

HE DO EVERYTHING BIG

s.l. simpson

"He dead?"

"You know he is."

Barker steps closer. He can see the boy, leaning away from him, eyes bulging out of their sockets, dried blood and brain matter splattered on the fabric roof of the silver minivan.

Barker looks at the shotgun, the boy's thumb still stuck in the trigger guard. An analog watch rests on his thigh, two small circles of dried blood over the three and over the six.

"He's a big feller ain't he?" Thompson says.

"Yeah, he is."

"And what you make of that?" He points at the watch, almost touching it, his sheriff's badge scraping past the nose of the dead boy.

"He watched the time. They do that."

"Do what?"

"Watch the time like that. They decide they gonna do it at say 12:30 p.m., and they watch and when that clock say 12:30 p.m., that's when they do it."

"You think it's that boy been missing all week?"

"I reckon, but I don't know."

They found the van by a creek in the Arkansas wilderness, hidden by a rocky outcropping, glistening with quartz and other minerals. The birds sing around them, around the death and the smell and the stillness of it all.

"Fuck, man," Thompson says.

"That boy thunder."

"You know he is."

They watch him move down the field, football tucked under one arm. He sticks his hand out, just like he saw on the television, and the free safety doesn't stand a chance.

Their helmets collide like rams, and the crack makes the other boys stop and look. Linemen disengage from their blocks and stand there, watching. A small boy says out loud, "Holy shit."

"That boy lightning."

"You know he is."

The free safety hits the turf, sending a cloud of black rubber and fake grass flying. The other boy, the thunder, he keeps going, never stopping—never thinking of stopping—until he is in the end zone.

"Everything he do, he do big."

"You know that boy?"

"That's my boy."

The other men watch this holy moment, offer their supplications with tears hidden in their eyes. Four years and it is Friday nights, and he becomes their boy, too. Ain't no one from Booneville like this, they say. Ain't nobody from nowhere like this. They pray about it. On their knees they pray about it.

Beau is one of them. In his grays and helmet, he's one of them. But then again, in a lot of ways, he is not. Coach tweets on his whistle, and the boys bend in half, reaching behind their calves, pulling themselves downward.

Beau sees the lineman behind him, barely stretching, his belly too big and his legs too rigid to clasp any further than his knees.

Coach tweets again, and the boys go upright.

"Win," they say, all together, and down they go again.

Beau watches the lineman struggle. Robert is his name, a sophomore, but the biggest kid they got in the trenches.

When Coach tweets, they say win. Over and over. All morning, he reminded them what they are there for.

"You think this is fun? This ain't fun. Nothin' fun about this. This all about Friday. This all about winning. Ain't a game. When I blow this whistle, you say win, cause that what we do. We don't do that, we wasting time."

"Win." Beau whispers it to himself. He knows winning isn't just on the scoreboard. It is in every movement. It is in every drill. Every moment on the practice field is designed around this concept. You win against your opponent. You win against your teammate. You win against your Coach. His father told him. He believed his father.

"Coach say to go half speed, you go full speed," his father once said. "He say walk through, you go full speed. Soon Coach just know, Beau don't got half speed. Beau don't got walking speed. Beau go boom, and that's all he go."

Beau likes that. They finished warm-ups with jumping jacks, and at each peak, with their arms in the air as if in celebration, they call it out together.

"Win, win, win, win." Over and over, until Coach blows his whistle, and the hitting begins.

In the dressing room, he checks his jawline in a small cracked mirror affixed to the back of his locker. He clamps his teeth again and again so the tendon rolls across his cheek like waves to the shore.

"Hey, Beastmode, what you doin?"

It's Teddy Graham. That's what Coach calls him. Teddy Graham.

"Olson look just like a teddy graham," Coach said. And the upperclassmen made him stand with his hands over his belly, just like the cookie, and they laughed. And Teddy Graham laughed too.

Olson's a lineman. A junior, short and fat, with a square head. He's naked except a towel, but he has the center open on purpose so when Beau turns to look Teddy Graham's balls are right in his face.

Beau doesn't say anything. He just looks at the balls and looks away.

Coach call Beau "Big Easy" sometimes because he's big, and he makes it look easy. Everyone calls him Beastmode, too. Beau doesn't think twice about the games the others play in the locker room. He pulls up his pants, claps Teddy Graham on the shoulder, looks him in the eye for a long time.

"Win," he says, then turns him lose. Teddy Graham just stands there with his dick out.

Beau studies the eagle—the War Eagle—painted on the rubbery latex coated cinder blocks on the back wall of the gym. "That War Eagle gonna fuck you up," he says, and he touches the black outline, follows it with a finger like he sometimes follows his lead blocker through a gap.

What is school spirit? He knows. It's when he lifts his arms in front of the screaming student body, and they say his name like they never say it any other time. It's when he steps across the goal line, and the nearest defender is 25 yards behind him. It's when a different cheerleader sucks him off every Friday night.

It's when Anna Carol don't, and suddenly she's the most beautiful and most sacred. He wants to hold her and put her hair between his fingers like the laces of a football and feel something soft and hear her little voice speak to him where only he knows what she says.

He swoops his finger around the outer circle of the War Eagle, following it inward across the wings, across the razor-sharp talons. "That War Eagle fuck you up," he reminds himself. "Fuck you up real good."

Barker stands in the driveway. There are cars everywhere. Thompson steps out of the patrol car, his boots crunching in the gravel.

"They come from everywhere," Thompson says, and he points at a license plate.

"Californy," Barker says. "Nice ride, too." There's a University of Southern California decal on the back glass. Barker sticks his thumb at it. "You reckon he here recruitin or here helpin look for this boy?"

They take a few steps toward the house—an old, green-painted thing, with white lattice and creeping ivy on the right side. Something stirs in the window, and Barker knows they are peeking out at him. He knows just by him being there they were already starting to panic.

"You remember him don't you?"

"Course I do."

"He ran 434 yards on 11 carries against Dover. That's a state record."

"Damn."

"Damn is right. Forty fuckin yards per touch, and you know he was on the bench by halftime."

"Probably."

Barker looks at the house. He rests his forearm on his pistol, leaning to one side.

"You tell them? Or I tell them?"

"You tell them. I reckon they know. He been gone a week."

"Kids go missin a week sometimes. Don't mean they dead."

"I reckon they suspect."

"Go knock."

Thompson tips off his deputy hat, draws in a deep breath. Barker does the same. They approach the house, which seems to sag under the weight of their burden, as if it knew.

"Ma'am, your boy, we found him. He's dead. We are sorry."

Barker stares past her into the living room. On the wall, the boy's high school jersey is framed. Another wall holds a life-size cutout of the boy, his arm extended toward a nonexistent defender, his leg kicked up in a high step, the football just barely visible in his right arm, tucked away like a child, safe from harm. The living room is filled with recruiters, their crisp polos showing their school logos. They are here, Barker knows, not to help find the boy, this woman's child. They are after their asset, for which they have already spent a considerable sum.

The woman screams. She screams like she'd done every Friday in the fall. She screams like every momma ever screamed when he told her what he told her. The boy's father takes her in his arms. He struggles to hold her on her feet.

"Stop it, stop it, stop it."

Barker doesn't know who he was talking to.

Anna Carol says she will go to lunch with him, and it's bigger than four touchdowns against Lavaca the night before. He types up the text three times before he hits send and flicks the phone into the corner of the couch, too scared to see her response.

When he does check, it says, "Sure."

Just that. "Sure."

Beau pulls on his favorite black and red War Eagles sweater.

"Sure," he says, grinning at himself in the mirror.

He brushes his teeth.

"Sure."

He tells his momma where he's going, and she smiles, too. He kisses her on the top of the head.

"Love you, momma," he says. She squeezes him tight around the torso. He gets his shoes from the front step, slides into them.

He takes her to Big Boy Burgers cause it's where he always goes. The old men in the corner get excited when he walks in the door. They're drinking soda and chomping on big greasy burgers and talking about the night before, 46-0 against Lavaca, and on their homecoming, too.

When he and Anna Carol sit, they stand and circle his table. Beau knew this would happen. It happens every time he comes here. It happens no matter where he goes. A small town like this changes during football season. Everywhere in town, every trip in Walmart—it's a tiny pep-rally, with Beau at the center. He smiles at her.

"Who's this pretty lady? This your lady? Shore is a pretty thing."

They all but pinch her.

"Just a friend," he says.

They share a glance, like they know something. One of them puts his styrofoam cup down on the table, puts both meaty hands down in front of them. He leans down, right in their face, and winks.

"Quite a show you put on Lavaca."

"Yes sir."

"Quite a show you put on Dover."

"Yes sir."

"You put a show on everybody so far."

"Yes sir."

"We gonna win state?"

"Yes sir."

"You got any offers? Where you going after high school?"

"Naw, just talkin."

"Where at?"

"Missouri, Arkansas, some D-2 schools. Some NAIA schools. Just talkin."

A murmur goes through the old men. Beau looks at Anna Carol, and she turns bright red. She cups one hand over her brow so they can't make eye contact.

"A boy like you do mighty fine at an Arkansas, I reckon. You win state, I reckon talkin become offers. You win state; it's all open to you."

"Yes sir."

After the men leave, Anna Carol tells him she hates football. She hates it. She takes a drink of her Dr. Pepper, looks at the old men who have returned to their slobbery burgers, and says, "I can't think of anything more pathetic than being grown and obsessed with high school football."

"War Eagle run deep," Beau says.

Her brow wrinkles up. "What'll War Eagle give you when it uses you up? What will you have left?"

"War Eagle will send me to college."

"Then what?"

"The NFL."

"I hate football."

"You don't know football. Don't nobody hate football. Why you cheer if you hate football?"

She thought for a long time. Longer than she thought before she said "sure" to having a burger with Beau at Big Boy on a Saturday afternoon. "Sometimes you ain't got a choice what you do."

"Why you come here with me then?"

Anna Carol shrugs. "I'll let you know when I figure that out."

Beau looks at the men, who seem to pause their entire conversation just because his gaze went their way. One man puts down his burger and gives a little salute with two fingers.

Outside on the glass, it says "GO WAR EAGLES WIN STATE" in red and black letters. The kids stop Beau and Anna Carol there, tugging on the sleeve of his hoodie.

There's six of them, all dirty and towheaded. The bravest one, a kid with blue eyes and an explosion of freckles across his cheeks and nose, speaks up.

"You the best player ever played here."

"Been a lot of good War Eagles."

"I'm gonna be just like you when I get big."

Beau gets down on one knee, looks the kid in the eye. Anna Carol just looks at them, bewilderment in her eyes. "Be better than me," Beau says.

The boy produces a piece of paper, folded into dirty sections. He opens it and hands it to Beau. It's a team roster from Friday's game.

"Sign it. When you make the NFL, I can show my friends."

"You show em. When I make it, I'll score a touchdown just for you," Beau says, scratching his name across his own printed name on the roster. "You keep that touchdown. Yours forever."

The boys giggle and clap the brave one on the back. Beau smiles at this. He can say do this, and they will. He can say do that, and they will. They look at him like he's already made it to the NFL, as if there is no doubt he will be there.

Anna Carol watches intently. She's lived here her whole life, but it's never been this serious. She had heard of the glory days, of the years her father spent playing at War Eagle Stadium, how reverent he is of those moments. Before Beau, her father's team had the best overall season record at 6-5. A record of 6-5, and the old man still can't stop talking about it. Maybe it's always been like this, she thinks. Maybe she's just never been in the center of it.

"This happen often?"

"You know it does."

"How often?"

"Every day. Football mean a lot to them. This the best season the War Eagles ever had. Ain't been a Beau Thurman before. They been good War Eagles, but they never been great War Eagles. Until now."

"You ever think of anything besides football?" she asks.

"Naw."

"Not ever?"

"Naw. Not ever."

"You might have something good to say if you did."

He looks at her, unsure whether he is insulted or not. He shrugs. He grabs her hand, and she doesn't protest. "I think about this," he says after a moment. "Doin this right here."

She blushes despite herself. He stuffs her hand and his into the pocket of his hoodie, and continues down the sidewalk. They don't walk a block without someone stopping them.

"Who's this pretty young thing on your arm?"

"This your girlfriend?"

"We beating Ozark Friday? How many you gonna score?"

"You got offers?"

"You gonna play for Arkansas? Fine school that is."

"I cain't wait to see you on play on Sunday."

They pinch and prod him. Children ask to feel his muscles. Women run their hands on his chest, feeling the shape and firmness—something none of them have ever felt in their own men. They giggle like high school girls. Beau smiles and nods and hugs and says "yes sir" more times than Anna Carol can count.

Coach makes the seniors stand up. The underclassmen look up at them in the center of a circle, the entire team on their knees.

"This is it," he says. "Ain't nothing but four quarters of high school football for these seniors. Ain't nothin left after that. This game ends for them. For most of them. These seniors deserve your best. They deserve that state championship. Ain't nothin matter in this whole world but winning this game. You hear that? Ain't nothin else that matter.

"But I ain't gonna lie to you. They got three D-1 kids at Warren. We prepared. All week we prepare, but those kids gonna come, and they gonna hit you in the mouth, and the question is, 'What are you gonna do about that?'"

He turns, looks at Beau, lets his gaze linger there for a long time.

"They got three of you," he says, slowly, like it's the most important sentence he's ever said in his life. "They got three of you, and what are you gonna do about that?"

"Ain't three of me alive," Beau says, and the team cheers. They get hyped. They link arms, and they sway together like tribal warriors preparing to take the battlefield. Beau beats on his chest with a fist. He slaps the helmets of his teammates. He tugs on their shoulder pads. They tangle with each other until the aggression and anticipation has built to a frenzy, until it is tangible among them. Until Beau can taste it on his lips.

"You will punish them for lining up against you," Coach yells. "Punish them."

Beau is still thinking about that word when the War Eagles burst on the field. He rolls it around in his mouth, feels the popping of his lips and the lifting of his tongue as he whispers it to himself. Punish. He stares across the field until he can see the orange and black uniform of the Lumberjacks. He watches them warm up, and it is offensive to him.

Beau takes the opening kickoff 99 yards untouched to the end zone, and they light off fireworks behind the goal post. The scoreboard flashes, and the students scream, "WAR EAGLE, FIGHT, WIN." He jumps into the stands, feels their hands around him, grabbing at him, pulling him in all directions.

Coach puts him at linebacker on defense, and he prowls back and forth before the ball is snapped and he is loosed from his cage. He tears through the line, sees the handoff and sends the kid flailing to the grass. Beau stands over him, daring him to stand, too late to see the quarterback has pulled the ball and flung it to a wide open receiver for a touchdown.

"Stay home," Coach says, slapping him on the helmet. "Beau, they readin you. Stay home. Make the quarterback make a decision."

Beau gets stood up by the left tackle, and they stare at each other like two lions tangled up in the savanna. For a moment, the chaos around them vanishes, and they are alone together.

Beau puts the lineman on his back on the next play and hits the quarterback. He presses the boy's head into the ground and screams into his helmet. "You ain't nothin."

Coach still yells at him on the sideline. "Ain't I just said for you to stay home? They reading you Beau. Just you. They don't gotta beat us, Beau. They just gotta beat you."

Beau can't stay home. He sees the play, and he sees no one else can make it. When he stays home, the running back gashes them for four or five yards at a time.

With 1:12 left in the fourth, the War Eagles are down 41-35 with one timeout. Beau runs two times in a row for nine yards. Coach calls a bubble screen that goes nowhere, and suddenly it's fourth-and-1 on the War Eagle 45.

"Up the gut," Coach says. "Do it. Just get the first."

"Yes sir."

They line up fast, trying to save their timeout. Beau takes the handoff. He can hear them in his mind.

"Beau bring the boom."

"That boy lightening."

"That boy thunder."

He can hear them speak, their voices, the creaky violin seesaw way they talk, whispering behind his ear.

"You gonna win state, boy. You gonna go to Arkansas. You gonna be in the NFL."

He lowers his head. The force hits him like God himself says no, and he goes nowhere. He tries to bounce outside, but they have him, a hundred hands pulling at his arms, his legs, his jersey. He slips. His knee hits the ground.

They are already celebrating on the Warren sideline. And Beau knows.

He can hear Coach say somewhere in his memory, "You think this is fun? This ain't fun. Nothin fun about this. This all about winning."

Anna Carol sees him pacing in her driveway. She doesn't know why, but she looks out the window, and there he is. Pacing.

She watches him, hands stuffed in his War Eagles hoodie, shoulders hunched. She goes to him, and on the front porch he glances at her, like he's surprised, as if he didn't pace in her driveway for this express purpose.

"You all right?"

"I am."

"Then what you doing figure eighting in my driveway?"

"I just come here. I didn't know where else to come."

He stops walking, looks at her. She sees he is hiding tears and realizes she has never seen a man cry in her life. Something breaks in her. It isn't natural. When she touches his shoulder, he can't hide it. He sobs. He puts his head in her neck and cries.

At the diner in town, the glass that once said "GO WAR EAGLES WIN STATE," now says, "1:12 SHORT."

"Ain't no one say even hi to me today," Beau says. "Won't even look my way."

She thinks about telling him it is silly to cry over football, that by tomorrow no one will remember the semifinals of the state championship. But she knows she is wrong. They'll remember. They'll never forget.

She leans forward and kisses him, soft at first. He seems unaware of what is happening. Their tongues mingle for a moment, but he pulls away, and she thinks she has solved it. She knows what he needs to hear, what he hasn't heard, what fathers and grandfathers and old men at diners and little children asking for autographs and newspaper articles never once said.

"There is more to you than football," she says.

He looks at her. For a long time, he doesn't speak.

"Beau was a record breaker," the school superintendent says, lifting his hand in the air. "Beau started as a freshman, and he rushed for 14,364 yards. A school record. He has a school record for most yards per attempt in a game, almost 40 yards, most touchdowns in a game, seven, most in a season, 41, and most in a career, 140. And I want you to remember he was on the bench by halftime almost every game. Beau lived in that end zone. He lived right there in that end zone."

He points past the metal folding chairs, the flowers and the casket on the 50-yard line of War Eagle Stadium. "On Fridays, that end zone was Beau's home."

Close friends and family sat on the field. Fans sat in the stands. A group of linemen carry his coffin to the end zone for one more touchdown as the high school band played the fight song. The fans cheered like they weren't at a funeral. Beau's father falls on his knees.

"Beau was the guy on another level," Olson says when it's his turn to speak. "He that guy goin somewhere. He wasn't like me, and he wasn't like any of us. Beau picked up tractor tires after practice. After I gone home. After I ate. When I was goofin off, Beau was there, flippin those tractor tires.

"Before Beau, War Eagles was 2-8, when he was a freshmen—a little squirt—we went 7-4, then 8-3, then 11-1, then 13-1 and state runner-up. Every year he grow, and we grow too. I think about 1:12 in the fourth quarter against Warren damn near ever day. I think about how he just need that one yard and from there who knows? Who knows if I block my man a little better what Beau make happen. But there was only one of Beau and 10 of us."

Teddy Graham kisses the coffin, puts his hand on the polished oak grain, and cries hard. The stadium is quiet—silent like it's fourth-and-1 in the waning moments of the state championship, and Beau has the ball.

DROPPING DIMES

chloe n. clark

There was barely anyone on the highway. Tony felt it was a mixed blessing: he wanted to need to pay attention, to not think about things other than working within the flow of traffic, but he also wanted to get there quickly. He remembered something a teammate, Liam, had once told him: to be good, you have to always consider every possible outcome, but not expect any of them. Tony had thought, at the time, like it sounded like the kind of pseudo-philosophic crap that people spouted when they wanted to sound like they were saying something complex. Years later, though, and Tony had understood it. It was about knowing what could happen, every possibility, but preparing for there to be something, something probably worse, that you'd been unable to imagine.

"What the fuck?" Marissa had been naked, hair still dripping from the shower. "Seriously. What. The. Fuck."

In his head, Tony ran through all the possibilities that could've made her jump out of the shower to yell at him. There weren't many answers to the equation. "Uh?"

"Your phone. Your fucking phone." And then he noticed it in her hand, as she jabbed it at him accusingly. He must have left his phone in the bathroom, sitting on the counter, allowing it to do something that turned Marissa into a wet ball of rage.

"My phone did what?"

"No putting the blame on your phone. My phone did it. It wasn't me." Marissa shoved the phone at him. Instinctively, he grabbed it. There were seven missed calls. All from Gia.

"Whoa, whoa, Riss. This isn't what you think," he began.

Marissa was already turning back to the bathroom. "What am I thinking? Because what I had been thinking was that you told me you talked to her about calling us. About asking for things."

"I didn't start this. I didn't call her," Tony said. But he could already feel his fingers itching to hit the Call Back button.

"But, you're going to call her back. You're going to get her out of whatever shit she's in. And we're going to be down… Whatever. Money. Sanity. Time. Whatever she needs." Marissa's shoulders slumped, the rage leaving her body. She stepped into the bathroom, quietly shutting the door, before he could answer.

When she was five, Gia saved Tony's life. He was one, crawling on the floor and popped a button in his mouth. His mother, on the phone, never saw it. Gia did. She was playing with her Barbie and saw him cough, go red. She ran to him and copied something she had seen on a TV show that she probably wasn't supposed to be watching. The button came out. Tony lived. Their mother swept them both into her arms.

The story was so intrinsic to their family, so trotted out at every gathering, that Tony could picture it even though he had no memory of the event. In his mind, he saw himself on the floor. He saw Gia run to him, acting so quickly that it seemed as if she was possessed. What five-year-old knows to perform the Heimlich? Knows to do it so gently that the baby is unharmed? He saw the button fly, black and shiny with spit, through the air. And Gia held him for a moment longer as he burst into infuriated squalls, as his mother ran to them.

Tony always thought of the button first whenever he thought of Gia. In the hospital, after one of her events, he would think of the button as he talked to the doctors. He would think of the button as he signed papers, agreeing to pay her bills.

His sister was not a healthy woman. Not sound of mind, their mother said. She said that was a kinder phrase than "mentally imbalanced." When Tony was a teen, he pictured the phrase as someone tapping on Gia's head with a little drumstick. The sound it made was like a shrieking, like the clattering of a glass falling into a sink.

"Hey, Tony, Tony, Tony," her voice was high, breathing clipped.

"Gia," Tony said.

"I called you, you so many times. Ringing and you not picking up," Gia accused.

"I didn't have my phone on me, Gia. What's up?" He kept his voice calm, breathing in and out loudly so that she could hear how breathing was supposed to sound.

"You need to pick me up." Gia never phrased requests as if they were her own. "I'm at this hotel, no motel, no. Wait. What's the difference? Which one is 'h' and which one is 'm'?"

"Well, the 'm' has three curves down and the—" he began.

She laughed. Her laugh was disorienting: like someone screaming but thinking they were having a good time. "Shut up. I'm at the one where you pay by the week and the soap isn't fancy, it's just those little white blocks and there isn't even a name on it. Like it has no brand?"

"I think that's a motel, Gia."

"Well, then, I'm at a motel and you need to pick me up."

"I didn't even know you were in town. But okay." It was easy enough. He'd pick her up. He'd take her to their mothers. Then they'd decided whether she needed to be checked in somewhere.

"Okay, good. I'll wait here." Her breathing was still rushed.

"Now what's the name of the motel?"

"It's called the Ames Inn. Inn! That's it. It's not a hotel or a motel. An inn." So pleased. Her breathing slowed finally.

"Ames?" Tony could already hear Marissa. The way she'd say his name, the mix of sadness and anger. "As in Ames, Iowa?"

"Yeah. Duh. Where'd you think I was?" Gia began to hum.

"I... I thought you were in Madison. Here. Home."

"Why'd I need to be picked up, then? Sometimes you're just so dumb, Tony. I hate to say it, you know I love you, but it's like you don't have any sense." Gia sighed. In another life, it would be fun to hear the exasperated older-sister-tone in her voice. In another life.

"It'll take me a bit to get there. But I'm on my way. Just stay there." He hung up. He wondered about calling his mother. Then he thought of how drained she had looked over the past few years—the way her strong jawline

{48}

had been so permanently set into a frown that it now looked more severe than majestic, the white that creeped into her hair. He'd call her once he knew what was what.

The drive was almost five hours and it was already three PM. He thought about just leaving Marissa a letter, letting her come home to him gone and a sweet note. But, he thought there was a good probability that he'd come home to divorce papers, his key no longer opening their front door, even a slight chance of his clothes sitting out in the parking lot. So he left her a voicemail, instead.

He'd been to Ames a few times. Back in college, they'd played against the Cyclones a few times. He never quite got the team mascot: a bird named after a tornado. Shouldn't it have just been a personified tornado? That would've made more sense. In the Sweet 16 the year of the Final Four, he'd even become friend with the Cyclone's point guard—Marcus. He liked that about basketball; it always seemed less antagonistic than other sports.

Marcus wrote him a long e-mail after the loss, later, said some kind things that he seemed like he meant. Tony had appreciated the thought, the general decency, but had never written back. Not out of choice, but out of Gia. By the time, she'd gotten through the flip-out she'd been working on, it felt weird to write back.

The drive was easy enough: lot of flat, flat, flat, and then some fields. He stopped in Dubuque for gas and a chalupa from Taco Bell. It tasted like salt, grease, and things he'd rather not think about. The sky was already going dark and he still had three hours to go.

He wondered what some of his former teammates were doing with their lives, he'd fallen out of touch with so many people over the years. Marissa had kept in closer contact with some, the other player girlfriend's she'd been friends with, but she rarely spoke about them—other than an occasional did you hear Lonna Blake had a baby? or have you seen how chunky Gretchen Iles got? She was so fucking skinny. And now look at her!

Out of the corner of his eye he saw the bridge, lit up and filled with a slow progression of rush hour cars. The way the lights bounced down to the water below made him think of gemstones.

Tony was seventeen, the first time that Gia threw herself from something. She'd been acting strange that whole year, even before having graduated from college in the spring. Gia, up to that point, had just been his big sister—sweet, feisty with their mother, gregarious. There'd been signs of trouble that they never really thought to much of: a penchant for strange dreams, screaming nightmares more than occasionally. But nothing that seemed worrisome, nothing that seemed serious.

Later, her college roommate would tell them how she'd found Gia one morning weeping in their kitchen. Her whole body was shaking, and she was pounding on the floor, so hard her hands were leaving bloody marks. I thought she was possessed.

He was practicing his jump shot in the driveway, when his mother came running out. She was a beautiful woman, stately some people called her, but in that moment she looked like she'd been dead a week and had just crawled out of her own grave.

"Mama?" he said. And, even years later, he would remember how soft, squeaky his voice came out.

"We've got to go, Tony. Gia… She…" His mother shook it off, went to the car, and he followed her.

They didn't talk the whole drive. His mother clutched the steering wheel, knuckles so white that they didn't look like they could belong to the rest of her body. Tony felt his stomach clenching up, worse than the worst gas cramps he'd ever had. He'd get used to the feeling, eventually.

The bridge wasn't a particularly tall one and the river wasn't one that rushed and raged. Still. It was a bridge. It was a river. There was a drop from one to the other. Gia was on the railing, standing up, her feet bare, toes curled slightly around the metal bar. People were all around. A cop car had its lights flashing, though the siren was off.

They got out of the car and ran up to the bridge.

"Gia!" His mother yelled. "Gia!"

Gia didn't turn, she pushed herself upwards, almost on tiptoes. It'd've looked almost extraordinarily impressive and athletic if it wasn't so bottom-of-the-stomach frightening.

"Gia… " Tony meant to shout, but his voice came out a whimper.

Still Gia heard him, she turned. A skillful spin. "Save me," she said.

And then she leaned backwards and was gone.

Tony's phone rang. He glanced at the Caller ID: Marissa. Pulling over, he answered. "Hey."

"Tony." She said his name like it was an elongated sigh.

"I'm sorry, babe. I can't not." They'd had the fight a few times. Marissa had loved his sister at first, during Gia's good years. Gia would visit and do Marissa's hair. The two of them like sisters, giggling and gossiping.

The first time there was an episode, Marissa had cried. She'd been so worried. The second time, she'd still cried. By the seventh, when Tony was at another hospital, talking to another doctor about why his sister wouldn't stay on her medication, Marissa hadn't even come with him. Tony, she needs to take her pills. To have some goddamn accountability. It's not just her life. There's you and your Mom and Gia acts like a child refusing her fucking penicillin.

"You have to stop, Tony." Marissa's voice shook. "She's your sister, but she's never going to stop ruining your life. She's like a walking emergency room."

"She's my sister, Riss. That should be enough for you," he said.

"One day, you're not going to get there fast enough. You know that, right? One day you're not going to save her and you're going to feel so guilty and it will break you and she won't care. She'll be gone and she won't care what she'd left behind." Marissa's voice cracked, congested sounding, weak.

Tony hung up.

"They make me dream in black and white," Gia had said. Tony was twenty and it was basketball season and he needed to get out on the court for practice or coach would cut his minutes.

"What do you mean?" he asked.

"The pills, they take all the color out of my dreams and, sometimes, Tone, I'm walking outside and I think I hear something. It's like a car beeping, you know, like when you left your keys in the ignition and it's that beep beep beep? And then I realize that its birds singing and their songs sound mechanical and I know that it's the pills. That they're slipping into reality and they're draining every day, too, and not just my dreams. Do you know what I mean?" Gia's voice sounded like an empty room: hushed but waiting to be filled with life.

Tony wanted to answer her right. But he saw a teammate, Liam, poking a head into the locker room, eyes worried. Liam motioned with his head, a single jerking movement, for Tony to get out there.

"Gia, I'm going to think about that. I'm going to see if I can figure out what you mean and then I'm going to call you back, okay?"

"Okay, brother. Call me back. Play hard. Win games. Be exceptional." It used to be a joke between them: who could say the most platitudes at the end of phone calls.

"Love you, sis," Tony said.

"Love you, love you," she replied. He didn't know if she was still playing the game.

It took him awhile to find the Ames Inn. The city was more built up then he remembered and the Inn was tiny, nondescript. He called her to get the room number but she didn't pick up. The cramping in his stomach almost didn't hurt anymore.

In the main office, the woman behind the desk looked like she belonged in a movie about stereotype librarians. She even had her glasses on a chain around her neck.

"I'm looking for my sister. She said she was staying here. Gia Carrola?" he said.

"She's in room eight. She's your sister?" The woman looked him up and down, not suspicious but something else.

"My big sister, yeah."

"Is she alright?" the woman asked. Her voice soft, worried, hoping to help.

"Sometimes," Tony said. He turned and left.

Room Eight was the last one in the first-floor hall. He knocked on the door.

Once, when he was twelve, he'd woken up to find Gia in his bedroom. She was sitting on the corner of his bed. It was before everything. When they were still just a normal family, or as normal as any families ever are.

"What's up?" he mumbled. He wanted to go back to sleep, go back to dreaming of the NBA team he'd one day play on.

"I had a bad dream. You were turned into a tree and I couldn't find you. I was in this whole big forest and there were so many trees and I couldn't find which one was you. Somebody had said you were a you-tree and that didn't seem helpful at all," Gia said. Her voice shook, like she was about to cry, but her face was dry.

"No, Gia, a yew tree. Y-E-W. It's a specific kind of tree. I know what they look like." He yawned, not covering his mouth.

Gia laughed, the shake gone. "Tony, I needed you in my dream. You could've helped me find you!"

He laughed, though he wasn't sure why. It was just like he needed to be laughing with her. She stood up, punching him once lightly on the shoulder, and then she left. He fell back into his dreams easily.

He knocked on the door. Gia opened it slowly. She looked worse than ever: hair unwashed and everywhere, the sleeves of her shirt were ratted from fretting, the skin around her eyes was so dark it looked like she'd been punched.

"You came," she said. She stood back, so that he could walk inside the room. It smelled like Gia had been there awhile: sweat and stale grease from leftover fast food. She walked to the bed and sat down on it. He followed her, sitting down on the very edge of the mattress. The blankets were strewn about in tangled heaps. It looked like she fought people in her sleep.

"What do you need Gia?" he asked.

She shrugged.

They sat in silence for a few moments. He noticed her fingers playing with something.

"What do you got, Gia?"

She held up a button. It was black and shiny and for some reason, if he had to guess, he'd say that it was the button from a coat.

He reached to take it from her but she shook her head. She opened her mouth and put the button on her tongue, like a flat piece of licorice. "Can you save me?"

He nodded and, so, she swallowed.

TWO STORIES

steve chang

Santa Fe Reservoir, 1996

Truth is I don't know if he *was* a friend.

There's this photo of the homeboys at a BBQ at the Santa Fe Reservoir: the white sun is shining, the grills are smoking, and there's all this good food out and coolers of Coronas, and Lumpy says, Smile! and all of us repping in gray and black, the kids too, get together to throw up the hood and pose for it.

But him.

He's still sitting back there by the benches, his rotten arm tucked up in that rotten sling, and the one that didn't get hit reaching past *all* our plates to snag that last drumstick rattling in the bowl.

Look. I'm not talking about him snatching that chicken. That chicken is good. But check his face though.

While we're all happy and shit?

Only *he'd* look like that.

It all comes out, no matter how many years later.

He hated that photo, but it was telling the truth.

Halloween, 1992

Nobody said, Listen up, but when it was time to drop Dougie, we all knew. He'd been hanging around too much. He'd gotten too comfortable, laughing at his own jokes and arching his too-thin eyebrows.

He had to go.

We had him meet us at the park on 2nd, by the benches, where we silently gathered. Little Tim had swapped out his fat Adidas laces for skinny black ones. He tightened them carefully. We didn't bother dressing up or putting on monster masks. We were 13. We were what we were.

We'd told him the plan for Halloween—kicking pumpkins and snatching candy sacks from the kids—so he arrived ready for pranks, rocking a lit-up devil horns headband, and saying Boo! and laughing: at *us*.

This only confirmed our opinion of him.

At the first house, he ran up the porch steps before anyone and booted that pumpkin into pulp and shrapnel, always so eager, trying so hard.

While we walked away from the light, Little Tim said, Ay. You got pumpkin on my pants. Dougie was still laughing. Sorry. You see that though? That pumpkin fucking blew up.

Yeah, said Little Tim, blew up all over my pants.

Then he hit Dougie in the mouth.

Hey what the hell?

Timmy hit him again, and we circled the two, to keep the fight fair, we said. But Dougie didn't fight very hard. We didn't have to do anything. He dropped on his own.

We stepped away from him curled on the sidewalk: a spit-out thing. He didn't say, Fuck you guys, or ask why. He seemed to know. He must've been heartbroken.

These days, he works in sales. In his Facebook photos, he's always in suits, always smiling. In the end, he had turned out OK it seems, better than we had—just as we'd suspected he might all along.

SPARROWS

zsombor aurél biró

translated by timea balogh

Imi calls me up Wednesday to get drunk. We meet at Madách Square, but he's alone.

"The others?" I ask.

"They didn't show."

"What do you mean, they didn't show? We promised after our last withdrawals that—"

"They didn't show."

We leave it at that. We go into a bar. Imi buys the first round, four tequilas and two beers. I whistle. It's part of the pact that no one ask why the other wants to drink, but with such a heavy start I feel like it's necessary.

"Why are we drinking?"

"Because life is fucking great."

We clink glasses. Imi snorts, he doesn't like alcohol, which is partly why he started smoking way back when. Or because getting high as a bird is the best thing out there. Then came the rest. I don't know. We've never talked about it, that's part of the pact too.

"And what have you been doing since?" he asks.

"Studying."

"What?"

"All kinds of bullshit."

"Why?"

"I don't have anything better to do."

He nods. He gets it. I study, Csaszi is an alcoholic, Feri spends around eighty a month on weed, Nikó got fat. That's what happens when you come off it. His girlfriend's the only reason Imi's alive.

We leave after the next round of tequila because Imi says there's going to be a concert at Kuplung later. He has molly too, so we can really get wrecked. He offers me some, but I don't want any. If I'm gonna be clean once and for all, I'm gonna be clean. Besides, he invited me out to drink, so according to the pact I'm responsible for him tonight.

There aren't a lot of people at Kuplung. Imi disappears once we step inside, so I'm left alone with the empty tables and the lamps that hang from the taut wires around me. I can't even make it to the bar, I run into people I know right away. From Pázmány University. It's only nine o'clock, but they're wasted, they ask what's new with me. One of them heard I was able to come off the stuff. What's on the tip of tongue is call it by its name goddamnit, but Imi reappears with two pints of beer.

"What should we drink to?" he asks.

I look to the Pázmány's.

"To two years being clean!"

Imi laughs, it hasn't been two years yet, but whatever. One year, two years, five decades. It doesn't matter. We ditch my old classmates and sit down under the lamps. Imi's rolling, talking about something I can't follow. Old times, I guess.

"What are we doing here?" I cut him off.

"You don't like this place?"

"I do. I just don't get it."

"This is where I first met Fanni."

"And?"

He gulps his beer.

"I asked her to marry me yesterday!"

I congratulate him, give him a smile, hug him. Nice job, thanks man, let's drink to that, I'll get the next round, etc. I go to the bar and order two whiskeys; if I remember correctly, Imi hates that the least. Meanwhile I'm thinking about how this is what a rehabilitated heroin addict should look like. Not like me, or the others. Imi has a job, money, a fiancé. In short, a life. It's all worked out for him. Of course, it all depends on your perspective. I'm alive, so if we look at it that way, it worked out for me too.

"Prost!" I sit back down at our table and raise my glass.

"What?"

"Cheers, in German."

"Why the hell do you know German?"

"Why not?"

"Touché."

I'm just beginning to enjoy Imi's company when the Pázmány's come over. They congratulate me again for being clean and with that they settle down next to us. Newly rich imbeciles, one of them's bragging about his job, the second about his thesis, the third about how you can't find a hotel for under thirty-five euros a night in Dublin. I don't care to listen to them, so I motion to Imi for us to get out of here. He misunderstands me. He finishes his whiskey and burps in the face of the guy sitting next to him.

"Get out of here," he says calmly.

I hold my head in my hands, but it's too late. The guy acts indignant, beats his chest, and because Imi doesn't move, the guy gets brave, though he'd be better off dipping out. Of course, there's no way for him to know what's coming. He hasn't seen Imi on Bethlen Gábor Street punch his dealer in the back of the neck because he found cheaper heroin at Mátyás Square and realized that his dealer had been ripping him off for months. And now the MDMA is coursing through him too. I reach over the table and grab his arm, but he sweeps it away. He gets up and punches the guy in the gut. The others lunge after him and I step back because I know he'll take care of them too. Luckily the bouncers show up and kick him out before he can cause an even bigger scene. I follow them out reluctantly, it's not like I can say anything to absolve Imi, like sorry, my friend is drunk. All of Budapest is drunk, and yet only he starts fights.

"What was that?" I ask as we trot along Király Street.

"The kid pissed me off. He was spitting bullshit."

"You didn't have to beat him up for that. You're always spitting bullshit."

"You can go to fucking—"

"Why, you think it's okay that your girl agrees to marry you and the next day you're in jail?"

"She didn't."

I stop in the middle of the road. Some tourist runs into me. He yells at me, and I send him to hell in English. Imi looks up at the starless sky a little ways away.

"Didn't you ask her to marry you?" I walk up to him.

"Yeah."

"And she said no?"

"Yeah."

"You could've told me that sooner. I wouldn't have bought all that whiskey."

"You're nice."

"I could've bought twice as much vodka."

"You can now," he says, and heads for a bar.

We get drunk quickly. We're systematic, like back in the day, only now there's no flickering guilt that we're inching towards death. The bar is quiet for eleven, despite the fact that it's full. Imi's talking about his girl, whose name I can't even remember. I'm thinking about how strange it is, back in the day we kept a list of each other's girls and then analyzed the likelihood of whether one of them had AIDs. We had to because we shared needles. Now I can't even remember this one's name. Not like Imi's bothered, he's painting a vivid picture of how he prepared for the big moment. A movie at an independent theater in the afternoon, then dinner by candlelight at Pomo D'Oro, then a walk along the Danube with a bottle of wine. Everything was going according to plan, except for when he got down on one knee. The girl started crying.

"She was planning to break up with me that day," Imi says.

"And did she?"

"No," he chuckles. "I got up and left her there."

"Like a real man."

"Why, what would you have done?"

"I don't know. Maybe cried a little. Or shot up."

Imi doesn't say anything, just nods like, you see. I bite into my fried chicken sandwich, but then I remember something, and the bite gets stuck in my throat.

"Imi," I falter, after I've coughed myself to tears, "you didn't?"

"Didn't what?"

"You didn't shoot up after, did you?"

"Shot up, my ass."

"Good."

"I'm clean."

"It's not worth it any other way."

"It didn't even come to mind."

"Don't let it."

We drink. I slow down, I can feel I've had enough. Not Imi. The bar closes at two, the bartender lets us stay until three then kicks us out. I buy a vodka and head towards the tram, but Imi calls after me, says let's go down to the Danube. Let's go, it doesn't matter to me. I have just as much work to do tomorrow as any other day, I can stare at the walls of my apartment hungover, too. Imi doesn't say anything, just walks with huge steps and cranes his neck left and right. I remember the time he walked down Rákóczi Street just like this, asking every passerby if they had any heroin. None of our connects were coming through and he needed a hit; he would've asked a cop if he would've crossed paths with one. Now he's looking for a fight. I envy him. At least he wants something.

By the time we get to Bajcsy Street he grows bored of looking. He starts talking about rehab, about his memories of the last times we did heroin, the stupid fucking psychiatrist who Csaszi slept with at the end. And then he's talking about Csaszi, how he was never even our friend, only hung around us for the heroin, because he was broke and we always shared with him, and now where is he when we need him, he can't even keep the pact. I say he's probably lying somewhere drenched and drowning in his own puke, that was his ideal night back in the day too, shooting up and passing out with a needle in his arm for six, seven hours. Imi laughs. I ask him, why, were we any better? But suddenly he shouts, "Fucking Americans!" And he runs toward the Parliament.

Drunk tourists stumble around before the fountain on Kossuth Square. Two girls and two guys. They can barely stand on their own two feet, they're trying to take pictures with the Parliament in the background when Imi goes after them. He smacks the phone out of the taller guy's hand, then punches him in the face and knees him in the stomach. The poor guy doesn't even have the time to scream for help before he's lying on the ground. Imi yells and looks for the other guy. The other one's stepping back, but his pride won't let him leave the girls there.

"I'm gonna kill you, you fat fuck!" Imi yells, and uppercuts him in the chin so hard it cracks.

The guy goes down, but Imi doesn't quit, he stands the guy up and keeps hitting him, his groin, his ribs, his everything. The guy's body goes slack, his head falls onto his shoulder, but Imi doesn't care. He yells at the screaming girls to shut up and gets back to it.

"Go and fuck yourself, you piece of shit! You come to Budapest, huh? You cocksuckers! You come here because the beer is cheap, and you scream into the night with your lousy accents? What's your accent worth now, huh? What the fuck is it worth?"

And he hits him, and he would keep hitting him if I wouldn't go over there and grab his arm. Imi turns around, almost comes at me, I'm ready to headbutt him if I have to, but his eyes find mine, and he calms down. I tell him we should go, because the cops will be here any minute, and he wheezes and follows me down to the shore towards Jászai Square. We cross Margit Bridge without a word. Imi's wiping his bloody fists onto his clothes and panting like some rabid dog. He changes course at Margit Island and doesn't respond when I ask him where he's going. I run after him, follow him to the shore.

"Did your girl leave you for an American?" I sit down next to him on the cold stones.

"Yeah."

I nod. The sky is clear, the moon is white. What I'd give to shoot up right now. Across from us is the dug-up Danube shore, backhoes and brown mounds. Even taking a hit from a light bulb would be something. A drop of blood lands next to my foot. Imi's nose is red, it looks like they nailed him with a punch. He rips a leaf off the branch above our heads and blows his nose into it. He flings it into the Danube and stares with a glassy gaze at Árpád Bridge and the ship swimming towards it. Written on the side of it in about thirty languages is the phrase "See you later."

"Let's shoot up," he says.

I'll EXPLAIN THERE WAS A WAR ON

erick brucker

My grandfather used to ask to see my cigarettes. "Get the bell," he'd say, turning the pack over in his hands, "it's pell-mell." Then he would smile and ask if that commercial was still running, even though he knew it wasn't. He had quit smoking before I was born, but he still asked how my cigarettes tasted, if my brand still burned as slowly as he remembered. After the revolution, he was ashamed to have been drunk with Hemingway because, he said, men shouldn't associate with Communists. Then he got cancer. Then he died.

I had a close friend named Jason who gave me a bottle opener keychain of a menorah with some Hebrew words and dates on the back, none of which I understood. He had stolen it from a friend of his, and he gave it to me because I was practicing Judaism at the time. It was a Yom Kippur present, which is thoughtful. Jason still records heavy metal riffs he's written and sends them to me in text messages, but he turns the gain up so loud I can't make out a note.

My mom tells me that all the men who ever hurt her—her father, her first husband, my father—were smokers. She asks how both of her sons became smokers. She thinks that if I were a daughter, I wouldn't smoke.

She used to say that any son of hers would speak Spanish, so she wouldn't feed me until I could ask in Spanish. But I was already seven years old so I just made my own dinner. Years later, after I had learned Spanish, I realized that she didn't cook.

Jason had worked as a mall security guard until he got fired for terrorism. He had actually just typed some Slayer lyrics into a blank email and accidentally sent it to the corporate office, but the bosses called it terrorism because there was a war on. There was a group of us that, when one of us lost a job, would all go in the woods and drink as though it was the only way to make the sun come up.

It must be fifteen years since I've seen my brother go an hour without getting high. He keeps a one-hitter in his pocket and drags off it whenever he's outside or in the car. When he got back from Iraq he became a libertarian. Now he says that if a man wants to marry a man, or a duck, or a shoe, that's no one's business. He says he doesn't remember how many times he was shot at or blown up in the war, and why would he try to.

After his dad killed his grandpa, Jason joined the army. He never saw combat. He was discharged when he couldn't stop pissing himself in bed. He told me it was because of a kidney infection, but his third Steel Reserve told me he was killing himself every night in his dreams. In both cases I told him he should get checked out. Then we drank until the sun was up.

MISSING SAINT

scott daughtridge demer

Mark slumps in the dark corner with his legs pulled up to his chest, flicking a lighter. The flame stands for nearly a minute, brightening his face, then he presses the hot metal tip into his palm. His skin sizzles. He holds his eyes closed and hums a song.

I stretch out on the splintering pieces of plywood covering the floor. The walls are shredded Sheetrock, faded floral wallpaper, exposed two-by-fours. Splintered wood, glass, and ash litter the space from wall to wall. Birds had come in through the destroyed windows and dropped their shit and feathers all around. The smell of the honeysuckle vines growing over the trees in the backyard blows through the house, blending with the sweat and smoke coming from Mark's clothes.

I gather wood splinters and set my lighter to them. Mark looks at the water stain constellations on the ceiling. I blow on the flame, but it fades into a smoldering, flameless pile.

Mark was born in this house, lived here until he was seven years old. After Mark's dad died, Uncle Bibby moved in and helped raise Mark. He taught Mark to be polite to people, how to sew, play guitar; also taught him how to throw a punch, fix an engine, load a gun, which Mark has in turn taught me over the years. Without Uncle Bibby, Mark might have run away or starved by now. It's been three weeks since Uncle Bibby disappeared and Mark is already skinnier. His torn jeans and Dead Kennedys T-shirt hang off him like raggedy drapes.

Earlier in the year Mark got suspended for selling his Ritalin to Matt Harding. Mr. Werner, the principal, saw Mark hand the pill to Matt on the sidewalk behind the gym. Mr. Werner told Mark's mom he would reduce the length of the suspension if Mark attended drug education classes at the

Family Center, but she couldn't take off work from Bernie's BBQ to get him there. Uncle Bibby, who lived in the next county over, drove Mark to the classes so he'd only miss ten days of school. And even though Uncle Bibby smokes weed—Mark and I found a shoe box sized plastic container filled with joint roaches under his bed once—he told Mark not to do that dumb shit at school again and Mark said he wouldn't.

The house has been empty since Mark and his mom moved all those years ago and is now a strange temple for anyone who wants to slip between the cracks. It's mostly the tattered and stained kids with lip and eye brow piercings, and the scarred, gang initiated guys from our school who come here to smoke stolen cigarettes, drink warm liquor from plastic bottles, and fuck on discarded scraps of carpet found behind the Big Lots. Witnessing the house's decomposition is like watching a swarm of bugs slowly devour a piece of meat. Small holes become big holes, major pieces shift, break apart, and melt into the earth.

Mark rolls his thumb over his lighter's wheel, making the sound of grinding teeth. "Let's go to my old room," he says. I follow him down the hall. The flooring sags and groans beneath our slow steps. A square of sunlight coming through the window shines on a wooden chair in the corner. The chair has no seat and the legs lean at a slight angle. On two of the walls, from floor to ceiling, words have been written in pencil. The lines dip and rise, the letters are different sizes, some are lower case, others randomly capitalized.

"What is this?" I ask. Mark rubs his face and eyes. The dirt packed under his nails spreads up his fingers like he's filled with soot.

"It's a prayer. I found it in a notebook somebody left here."

"Prayer?"

"It said the prayer is like a magnet. To bring people back."

I step toward the wall and touch the gray scribble.

"Can you help me finish? I've been here for two days and I don't think I can do it by myself."

Mark stares into my eyes. For all the time we spend together, we are normally side-by-side, walking through the neighborhood, sitting next to each other in the cafeteria, riding in the same seat on the bus. Mark's small mouth is closed and turned down at the corners. I glance to the floor. I almost say it's a waste of time, that prayers are bullshit, that it won't bring Uncle

Bibby back, but there's nothing else we can do right now. We've called Uncle Bibby's friends, gone to the bar where he works, searched through his trailer, and his truck. Found nothing. The police say they are searching for him, but still nothing. I'm afraid Uncle Bibby is dead, but I won't say that. As Mark's friend, the only thing I can do is follow his lead. And maybe I am wrong. Maybe Unlce Bibby is out there lost, waiting to be lifted from his feet and carried through the moon lit night, over rivers and concrete, through forests, between buildings, back to us.

I look into Mark's eyes. "Do you have another pencil?" I ask. Mark pivots and the sun light forces his eyes closed.

"No, but we can take turns." The pencil is pocked with teeth marks and worn to half its original size. The point is dull and the eraser has been rubbed off.

Mark drags the chair across the room and holds the pencil out.

"Are you sure? I don't want to mess it up." He thrusts the pencil at me. I try to see the burn on his palm.

"Just copy what I wrote on the other wall."

I take the pencil and he sits on the floor, blowing on his hand. I place my left foot on the edge of the chair's frame and try to stand quickly. The chair topples and bangs against my ankle. Mark stands and picks it up.

"Go slow," he says. "Use the wall to give you balance." He holds the chair while I place both my feet on it. I press the tips of my fingers against the wall. The chair legs, barely nailed into place, pop and lean sharply, but I balance at just the right angle and it feels stable enough.

The day Mark came back from his suspension he got in a fight with Ricky Tatton, knocking a chunk out of Ricky's eye brow, because he called Mark a faggot. Mark got so mad because Uncle Bibby is gay and Mark didn't want anybody saying anything that would offend his uncle. The year before, Jason Trendall called me a faggot and I said, "So what if I am?" then ran in a classroom when he came after me. Mark had called me a wuss when I told him about it, but my dad left when I was a baby, and I didn't have a tough uncle to teach me how to fight. One night, after we drank a couple of his mom's beers, Mark taught me how to make a fist and told me to try to bust the other guy's eyebrow open.

"That way," he said, "even if you lose you'll put a scar on him that will last forever."

The prayer is one sentence. Seventeen words long. Glancing over at what Mark wrote, I carefully shape each letter so I don't make any mistakes. I repeat the prayer on the same line until I'm stretching so far the pencil is barely clasped between my fingers, the letters barely legible, then I drop down to a new line and write the words quickly, clear and bold. My teacher once told us that the flap of a butterfly wing can result in a storm in another country and I think good. I hope this small action has devastating effects. The world right now is being changed because of us. Then, instead of an m I write an n. I stare at the mistake. I've ruined everything before it even took hold.

"I fucked up," I say, turning to Mark.

He walks over and examines it like a doctor looks at a bleeding wound. "It's fine. Just write over it and keep going. Be more careful."

I write even slower, trying to make each letter perfect, trying to keep my lines straight, but I misspell the words, the lines are crooked. With each letter the space to cover gets smaller and the prayer more powerful. The muscle between my thumb and first finger starts to cramp. I keep writing. I write faster and say the prayer to myself. At the bottom of the wall, I kneel down to fill in the space near the floor. It feels like a person is standing on my hand, but I finish the last line and drop the pencil. The muscles in my forearm shift back and forth as I knead them with my thumb. I roll my wrist around, bend my hand back and pinch the muscles until they loosen. Mark jumps on the chair, whispering the words to himself. The muscles in his arm flex as he presses into the wall. The chair does not budge underneath him, the words appear on the wall so quickly it's as though he is not writing them, but revealing them from under a thin cover. I sit hypnotized by Mark's motions. It's as though Mark has been doing this since the beginning of time, directing the lives of those on the outside using the prayers and invocations from an ancient notebook.

Mark reaches the floor and I think he's going to stop and tell me it's my turn, but he climbs on the chair again and keeps writing. Even though I'm sitting, sweat collects on my chest and trickles down my stomach. Mark's shirt sticks to his back. Outside, the tree tops move in the wind. The painted shut window overlooks the kudzu covered backyard. Bees and dragon flies zoom in and out of the shadows beneath the leaves. No buildings or roads are visible from this window and it feels like we've tripped into a dimension all our own.

When it's my turn our hands touch, mixing the sweat trickling down our arms. A smudge of Mark's blood is on the pencil. I don't wipe it off. I hold the pencil tight and let it sink into my skin.

While I write, Mark paces between the door and the window, nodding his head, dripping his blood on the floor, murmuring the prayer. The scraping sound of the pencil against the wall is like a whisper, like the wall is reciting the prayer. I say the prayer. This is our quiet chant. Both of us glow in the heat of the room. We step in Mark's blood and track it throughout the room with sticky steps. A blister on my index finger opens, puss leaks onto the pencil. If Mark is able to bleed for his uncle then I am too. It's Mark's turn, then my turn again. We shift our weight from foot to foot while standing on the chair to keep our legs from going numb. When I stop writing for a second the pain in my hand disappears only to return when I start again. It hurts so bad that for a second I expect my hand to just lock up and fall off, but I keep writing. We stretch, reach, crouch, bend. The words are repeated so many times they lose their meaning. It feels strange to say them. There is no point of reference anymore. My mouth is dry. It feels like I've run a hundred miles. At one point, I forget what I'm doing and I stand perched on the chair, frozen. The room begins to tilt like I'm on a boat in the middle of the ocean. I press my body against the wall so I don't fall off the chair. I feel my ribs and the bones in my hand. I keep writing.

The square of sunlight moves around the room, turns orange, then fades. Eventually, we stand in the dark, the walls completely covered. Our bodies throb like bruises after a fight.

Mark lights a cigarette he stole from his mom. The cold menthol bites my throat. I take shallow drags, so I don't get dizzy.

For days after, the rhythm of the prayer plays like a jingle in my head. I dream that I'm in a field, standing on the chair with burning grass all around me. I wake up hours before my alarm with the words pulsing through me. I hope they are moving through Uncle Bibby as well, bringing him back toward us. I imagine him walking through a silver moonlit field that extends forever in the darkness. I imagine him laughing at a joke he hears at a bar. I imagine him sitting in a trailer asking himself how he could have left Mark behind. I imagine him drowned in a muddy river.

One Friday afternoon, two weeks after we wrote the prayer, we go back to the house. All the shit and debris in the front has been cleared away. The broken pieces of glass are gone from the windows. The scraps of drywall have been pulled down. It looks like someone is trying to renovate the place.

"I've been coming here at night for the last few days," Mark sa ys. "Getting everything ready." He holds his breath, he grits his teeth, not letting the tears fall from his eyes.

The door to the room where we'd written the prayer can barely open because of all the moldy pieces of lumber, broken wooden furniture, smashed doors, stacks of ripped cardboard and yellowed newspapers. The ceiling is now covered with the prayer. I guess Mark climbed on the heap of crap and wrote it there. I feel left out, like somehow he thought I couldn't help him do what he had to do.

"Why'd you bring all this shit in here?" I ask. It smells like the earth threw up a load of moldy bile.

"The books says if the prayer doesn't work to make a large fire for the person, that it will draw them back."

"What if that doesn't work?" I ask.

"Then this is his funeral."

He sparks his lighter on a brown wool blanket crammed between two pieces of a broken door. He flicks it and flicks it and flicks it, but the lighter just sparks.

I hand Mark a blue lighter I found in the gutter outside my house. The flame stands ready with the first flick. He presents it to the blanket. The fire climbs over the furniture, setting it ablaze. I back up into the hallway. Smoke fills the room. The fire spreads to the walls, scorching the prayer we'd written. The words ride the smoke through the house and out the broken windows, floating further and further out into the world.

DO IT WITH GRACE: AN INTERVIEW WITH PORTUGAL. THE MAN

ryan w. bradley

Since 2006, Portugal. The Man has been making fearlessly evolving rock and roll. Each of their eight studio albums have shown passion, experimentation, and growth in equal measure. The four year gap between 2013's *Evil Friends* and 2017's breakout, *Woodstock* saw the band record a massive amount of material before scrapping an album they had dubbed *Gloomin + Doomin.* In the end, their choice to start over led them to the Grammy award-winning single, "Feel It Still" and a new level of notoriety in the music industry and among listeners around the world.

My introduction to the band came in 2006, due to our hometown connection. I was shocked to find a truly great band could come from Wasilla, Alaska, a place where it used to be easy to be from because no one had heard of it. Then the 2008 election happened and ever since, uttering the town's name has come with a lot of baggage. I'm hopeful that P.TM can change that. The band now calls Portland, Oregon, home, but they remain strongly connected to their Alaskan roots.

I sat down with bassist, Zach Carothers and guitarist, Eric Howk on a sunny southern Oregon afternoon at the end of August on a day where our air was finally clearing of wildfire smoke. My digital voice recorder had died a silent death and so I was using my phone to record the conversation and Zach seemed pretty chill with me making up answers for him in the event that the recording didn't work, but I'm pleased to say that it worked perfectly. Other than when a leaf blower drowned Eric out for a few minutes.

RWB: With writers we talk a lot about how place affects their work and you guys are so connected to place, not only Alaska, but Portland. How have those two places, living in Alaska and Portland and immersing yourself in them both, impacted the songwriting and how the band has developed?

ZC: I think it's pretty much everything, honestly. It's where we grew up. And it's also leaving it. I mean, Alaska is beautiful and there's no place like in the world, but it's very isolated. There's no outside culture, or there's very, very little outside culture. And so there's a lot of space to kind of get to know yourself and a lot of time on your hands. It was beautiful and it is inspiring, but it was also the fact that leaving there when I was 19 or 20—when I left and went down to the lower 48, as we call it—we moved to Portland, which was just a giant Mecca of music and arts and film. And so to just have so much there—and I didn't grow up with that so I wasn't jaded by it—I went to everything.

We were hungry. I was at a show every night or some kind of art gallery or seeing some movie. We were broke as hell, but that didn't matter. Then we went out on tour and just saw the world and it was all about being broke and seeing what we could see. Then we would take that back to wherever we were, and put that into context. And that's how we would write music and record it.

EH: Growing up during long winters twelve miles outside of a town of 1,200 people, I got pretty good at my instrument, but I didn't know what to do with it up there. I was trying to figure out schemes to make music into some kind of living. I was directing a pit orchestra for a theater company doing *Annie*. I kind of had this moment where I saw myself wearing socks with sandals, like with a baton. I didn't really know what I wanted to do.

I moved to Seattle pretty much right after high school. I was 18 and had a hundred bucks and a bass and a backpack. I didn't know what I was going to do, I didn't know anyone that was playing music down there. I just knew I had it in my head, at least like growing up watching *Hype!*, the Sub Pop documentary, and having this idea that Seattle's three blocks by three blocks and everyone's in a garage band, which isn't terribly far off since I was going there at the end of the 90s. But, kind of to Zach's point, $5 shows don't really happen where we're from and they happen every night [in Seattle]. And you're spoiled for choice in a town. So, it's the same kind of deal. And I got really lucky and fell into fell into a few bands along the way. That got me to test the touring waters and see a bit of the country. Being friends with Zach and friends with John [Portugal. The Man's singer] and kind of staying in touch, I knew that from the first year that they were a band, they were hitting it really hard, like just going full in and I would see MySpace updates from Germany and be like, goddamn!

RWB: You're talking about not having the same access to culture and one of the things that fascinates me about you guys is that you have a lot of integration of visual art, from the videos—especially with "Sleep Forever" — and John's art, these things are a big part of your identity.

ZC: It all came from two very specific places: Toy Machine skateboards and Ed Templeton, all the art side, and then Knik Kountry Video. They had the craziest fucking selection of movies. Super artsy, super fucked up cartoons. Like you're in the cartoon section and you're getting *Fantastic Planet*, *Fire and Ice*. You're lucky to find *Wizards* at a Blockbuster, but shit got dark there and we watched—I mean, it's long winters, after the sun went down there wasn't a lot to do. You kind of stayed inside and you'd watch TV, read, you play guitar, listen to music. So, yeah, Knik Kountry Video and Ed Templeton are pretty much the reason.

Personally when I first saw that Toy Machine shirt with the hands and there's the machine and it had, you know, eight fingers, I was like, *oh, you can do whatever you want.* You just use your imagination a lot. I remember John talking about art and just how we'd picture things. I remember listening to "Come Together" by the Beatles and trying to turn that guy that they're describing... like make a mental image of that, making that into some kind of weird cartoon, like the Ed Roth version of the guy from "Come Together."

That's how our brains were working. Feet down below his knees? Are you serious?

EH: Knik Kountry Video, man. *The Peanut Butter Solution.* Some weird Canadian cryptic shit.

RWB: A lot of bands work to what you're talking about, of getting to that point of "we can do whatever we like" over their career. Talking about the Beatles, it took them their entire career to get to that point of "screw this, we want to do what we want to do." You guys have always done that.

ZC: Yeah, we did it a little backwards. Now we're going pop, but it's not that we're trying to or anything or that we're trying to sell out or make money. We were always trying to write good songs. We just didn't fucking know how. People thought we were just a crazy experimental band, that's what's so funny about it. We didn't know how to write a smooth transition, we didn't know how to properly tell a story. There are people who can tell an amazing story and there are other people that are bouncing all over the place like *True Detective* season two. We just didn't know what we were doing, so that's what happened. We've just been trying to get better every time.

RWB: People are perceiving that you've gone more pop and maybe it's the perspective of having watched the growth of each album—and sure, "Feel It Still" is real hooky—but if you listen to *Woodstock* all the way through it moves in a way other albums don't. Maybe part of that is the influence of hip hop.

ZC: Rap rock kind of did a bad thing. When it first started and I saw Aerosmith and Run DMC I was like, *oh shit!* and then the *Judgment Night* soundtrack came out I was like, *oh shit!* and then I was all, *oh… shit…*

RWB: It turned into Kid Rock.

ZC: Yeah.

RWB: Listening to *Woodstock* there's still a lot of experimentation happening. There's still a lot of playing. You're not Weezer, writing notebooks full of like analyzing how hits are made. You're still feeling music and doing it your way.

ZC: It's a weird thing. We were just learning more, we were just trying to write better songs. You try to trim the fat. A lot of people that write eight minute rock and roll epics are like, *Oh man, I could write a three minute pop song no problem.* No you can't. It's so much harder. Try taking the craziest stories or the most beautiful story of your life and telling it in two minutes and thirty seconds. That's hard. And to do it with grace and heart, that's what we strive for. That's why I love Motown. That's why I love "Ain't No Sunshine," man. It's just over two minutes and it's one progression, and it takes me so many places, makes me feel so many things. It's simplicity.

EH: My takeaway as a new guy, with a little bit of an outsider perspective, I've always noticed that with records before *Woodstock*, there have been thematic elements. They've always been self-referential, whether it's a lyric or a theme or a hook that comes back, like "Plastic Soldiers.". What they've done with *Woodstock* has been referencing other peoples' art. The interpolation of The Marvelettes or the Richie Havens thing. It's taking that same approach, but bringing outside influence to it. I think it just makes it more interesting at the end of the day.

RWB: Not only does the album wear its influences, you guys also openly embrace crediting those influences. It's not, *oh, we're being original,* its, *we're building on something we love.*

EH: Couldn't have said it any better myself.

ZC: Yeah, for sure. That's very important to us. We're not all original. We listen to music every day. And it's all out there. There's only twelve notes, man. It's all out there in the ether. You just gotta put it together in a different combination.

EH: We met and started playing music together, just learning as many covers as we could.

RWB: That's what art is about, right? Art comes from other art.

ZC: Art should make you want to do one of two things: quit or get better. And that's how I feel every day.

RWB: Lately you've had native groups opening for you. You've really embraced representation and acknowledging cultural heritage everywhere you go.

ZC: It started off in Alaska. We were talking about there not being a lot of outside culture. The only little bit that we did have was Native Alaskan art and culture and I was fascinated by that. And John grew up really close to the small mushing communities, so he was really in that and I was next to it, but it kind of took us traveling around the world and seeing it's just fucked up. You have no idea. In textbooks it's Christopher Columbus and Cortez.

EH: I didn't learn about Pol Pot and Cambodia until the Dead Kennedys. It wasn't in our history books.

ZC: Absolutely. None of that shit is. It's fucked up how deep you gotta dig to find out about that stuff. So, it's been really amazing to learn on this tour. We went to Australia and found out the story is exactly the same. Like this cookie cutter recipe for colonization. So everywhere we're going on this tour we've had some people with some kind of notoriety, whether it's chiefs, chairmen, and presidents of local tribes come out. We've been able to talk to them and learn from them. And then we just donate some of our time. We've got a lot of people and a microphone. And if there's anything they want to say about any issues past or present, or some people sing or drum or dance. It's been awesome. There's been a whole learning experience for us with the crowd as well. And we're just basically acknowledging, remembering, and respecting, you know, the land that that we're on is theirs. They got fucked over and we can't change that, but we can still learn and we can still acknowledge that.

RWB: You're also addressing mental health issues on this tour, which is a very personal topic for me. I know that what you guys do comes with a toll, but having listened to the music, I feel that in some way it's been an inspiration along the way as well. Some of the songs feel like they've been very affected by mental health issues. Maybe not your own, but those you've seen around you, maybe both.

ZC: Yeah, both. I mean, for sure. What's crazy about it, as you know, is it's like disease, it doesn't just prey upon the poor or minorities. Everybody's got it. And the problem is so many people have felt like it's been shameful to talk about. I mean, you know, Alaskans, like unless you have a fucking bone sticking out of your arm, you don't really go to the doctor. You don't talk about your feelings. If I try to talk about my feelings to my dad—my dad's amazing and super supportive—but he'd just be like, *talk to your mom*.

EH: Rub some dirt in it and walk it off.

ZC: Yeah, walk it off, champ. And then there are all the people comparing things you are never going to be able to compare. I know people who've had horrible fucking lives. Like what my mom went through as a kid and she's a great and supportive person. Some people take it the other way. Some people have terrible childhoods and they lash out and do terrible things. Everybody's coming from something. You're never going to know their story. I look at people like Robin Williams who brought that much joy to the entire fucking world. Nobody is safe from it. And we're not healthy people. That was our main thing when we decided to team up with Keep Oregon Well. We are not by any means like a poster child for healthy mental states. Everybody has to learn how to talk... or don't, but try to listen to yourself and do whatever you need to do. And it's so specific, so different. Help out a friend, just be aware of it. And that's kind of the first step. There's no shame in talking about it. There's no shame in not talking about it. If you want to go seek help or you can find a friend, but look out for yourself and look out for the guy next to you.

RWB: Most people, at least people who follow the band, know the story of scrapping an album to eventually get to *Woodstock*. Did that have a psychological impact on the band. What was that like?

ZC: Just confusing and horrible. Honestly, making an album is very, very mentally unhealthy. It's not, *Great idea, Chet, throw some guitar on that. Where's the tambourine?* It's like, *Fuck you. You're an idiot. You don't know what you're doing, I hate all my friends, I hate myself, I have no good ideas. I'm shit at everything.* It's Wayne White, who was the creative director for *Pee Wee's Playhouse.* He's just an amazing artist. He put out a documentary called *Beauty Is Embarrassing* and John and I went and watched him. He was actually doing a tour through a mutual friend. We got to hang out with them and we watched a Q&A afterwards and somebody asked what the best part of the creative process is and he fucking nailed it. He's like, *I find no joy, everything from the beginning of a painting or a project to the end. It's all pain, self-loathing, self-doubt, it's horrible. It's horrible. But at the end, there's just this just this pinprick of a thing that I just need. It's not even good. It's not even that it feels good. I just have to do it.*

We have good days and bad days. You know, we have a lot of fun in the studios, we have a lot fights, but that whole process was crazy. I think it was more just really unbelievably heavy and soul crushing pressure. Because we had taken a long time on this album, we had spent way too much money on it. People were waiting on it and it's not that we weren't happy with it, but the world was changing at such a fast rate. We were just finishing up right when the primaries were kicking in, and we were like, *oh, my God, the world's gonna be different when we put out this album and that's fucking terrifying. So like, do we scrap it? We can't scrap it. We can't do that.* And then finally, we just did it. And luckily, it was cool.

That was mostly John. John's got no problem throwing shit away. I stress out about a lot. It's funny, John stresses out more about things that do not matter to anybody else. But something huge and he's just like, *whatever, we'll just trash it and do another album.* And it was by far the best choice we made. It was the right thing to do. It was just scary shit at the time. Looking back it's not that bad. Yeah, we were very stressed out for a while. And until you put out a record, when it's done, but it's not quite out yet, you're just thinking about everything you want to change. You just drive yourself crazy. But then you feel stupid because there are terrible fucking things going on in the world and you feel like an ass. Like, *oh, I make art*. It's stupid that I'm even worrying about this shit. But this is how humans are always going to be.

THE LEGEND OF JON BAMBOO

leland cheuk

Obscenely early. A shooting day, so I headed to the set. As I pulled my Tesla out of the garage, I saw a skinny old dark-skinned Asian guy wearing a plain white tee and cargo pants in my rearview. Had I called the gardener to come early?

But this gardener had the wrong tools. I rolled down my window and asked what he wanted. He didn't answer. His hands were behind him, like a kung fu master. His hair was cut very short, his face deeply lined. Squinting and blinking, he resembled an Asian Clint Eastwood.

I repeated my question.

"I'm Herbert Lin's father." He brought forward his hands, one of them gripping a sizable revolver. He pointed it through the window, inches from my face.

"Tommy Kok," he said.

Tommy Kok was Herbert's stage name. He was the mope who got stabbed to death by Ryan Driver on set over at Lust Definition DVD. Driver led the police on an all-day chase, and when he was cornered in West Hills, he threw himself off a cliff. I'd met Tommy once, before he started out. He told me I was his idol and that I was living his dream: doing porn and fucking hot girls. I told him to chase his passion. *Don't let anyone discourage you.* Isn't that what you're supposed to say? Oh, and I introduced Tommy to one of the directors at Lust Definition.

"I've got to go to work now," I said, my hands up. "People are expecting me. If you shoot me, you won't get far."

"I want to ask you some questions," he said, thumbing the revolver's hammer. "If you leave now, I'll just come back tomorrow. Or tonight. Or the next day."

"That would be tomorrow too."

He jabbed the barrel of the revolver, hitting my left temple.

"My face!" I shouted, rubbing the side of my throbbing head.

"You don't need a face for what you do."

I wished I had some fucking neighbors. Bad enough I had to work with so many of the drug-addled. Worse that there could be a completely psychotic mope waving around a prop samurai sword waiting to kill someone on set. I didn't want to come home and blog to my tens of thousands of fans that I was afraid of getting my brains blown out in my new 6,000-square-foot home in Woodland Hills.

"Get in," I said. "I'll answer your questions if you put away the gun."

And so we drove to the studio. Me and Tommy Kok's father. Me and this armed, angry dad. Hadn't done the angry dad drive in almost fifteen years.

"I've seen your films," he said. "*The Legend of Jon Bamboo.*"

Ah, my magnum opus. The plot goes: three beautiful babes (Sunrise Flowers, Hannah Rose, and Brooke Lee James) follow a treasure map that leads to an island castle off the coast of San Diego where I, the reclusive, titular, and preternaturally well-hung Asian lover resided.

"It's based on a true story," I said. "Do you know the legend of Dick Ho? He was supposed to be the first Asian male porn star in the seventies. Said to be longer than John Holmes! *The Legend of Jon Bamboo* won a lot of awards. Best guy-girl and FFM threesome 2012. I'm proud of that film."

"Shut the fuck up!" he shouted, loud enough to make me pee a little.

My hands, at ten and two on the steering wheel, began to shake. "I only met your son once. He said it was his dream to do what I do. I think we should let kids pursue their dreams, no? This was my dream. I mean, not this, with you in the car with a gun, but—"

"Herb was a smart boy. He was going to college at UCLA. He was an engineering major."

"My parents were similarly skeptical," I said. "Then they saw my house and my cars. Now my mom calls every week to make sure I haven't caught a disease yet."

Tommy's father shook his head. He wore white gym socks with black shoes. Never a good sign. Several very long whiskers sprouted from his Adam's apple. Grooming is so important. His lack of grooming and attention to conventions of fashion should have been immediate red flags.

"My son did whatever you told him to do," he said. "I found out from one of his friends that he went to Las Vegas to see you at your smut awards show. He drank with you. You gave him advice. You gave him a contact to the porn company. You told him you started out as a mope."

I was hoping he didn't know all that.

Back when I was in high school, my dad kept a locked suitcase in his closet that I pried open with a screwdriver. Inside, I found a VHS tape of a movie that starred Peter North. I thought: I'm going to be that guy. So I worked on my body. I was naturally well endowed. School wasn't my thing. I had lots of girlfriends. After graduation, I moved from Monterey Park to Van Nuys to be closer to the studios. At first, I'd be one of the tuggers in a bukkake, or the guy cheering the couple on while they fucked in a college dorm party scene, or the dude who stood around in a mask in a BDSM. Mainly, I was the guy who uploaded videos on the website, and cleaned the set afterward. Lube gets all over everything.

Needless to say, with Revolver Dad by my side, I wasn't feeling sexy as we pulled up to the set, a warehouse by the Van Nuys Airport. I was scheduled to film two scenes. A boy-girl and a mommy-daughter threesome. We got out of the car, and I headed for my trunk to get my yoga mat and saw that Tommy's dad was waving his gun around like an iPhone.

"Jesus Christ!" I said. "Put it away!"

"Relax, Howard," he said, sliding his gun back beneath his waistband.

The fucker used my real name. He had really done his research. I warned him not to use my real name in front of the crew and especially not in front of my sexy co-stars. Inside, the director, Mack Sinner, was in the kitchen, getting some coffee, while the crew was messing with the lighting on set in the loft space upstairs. We all know that set well, the bed with white sheets. The second floor windows had a nice view of the runways, but no need to marvel at that—we weren't shooting the view.

I told Mack I had a visitor.

"I'm Jon's dad," Tommy's father said.

Mack looked pleasantly surprised. "This doesn't happen often. Parents visiting the set. Jon never mentions his family."

"I bet he doesn't," said my hostage-taker.

My balls were officially feeling like empty coin purses. "Give me a thirty-minute warning before we shoot," I said to Mack.

Mack again looked surprised, but this time, not pleasantly so. The thirty-minute warning was industry-speak for "I need to pop a boner pill."

"You okay, JB?"

"I'm fine," I said. "Just had a hot date last night that lasted until morning."

Mack shook his head with admiration. "This guy gets as much pussy as the country of China," he said to Tommy's father. "You should be proud of him."

A look of nausea scrolled across his face.

I disappeared into the dressing room, unrolled my yoga mat, turned on some slow ambient EDM, dimmed the lights, lit some aromatic candles (lavender), and sat cross-legged on my mat in the middle of the room. Tommy's father perched on the folded-up futon and looked around before fixing his gaze upon the framed *Game of Death* movie poster on the wall (one of the producers bought me that for my last birthday). I wished now that it was one of Bruce Lee's more benignly titled works, like *Enter the Dragon* or *The Green Hornet*. I shut my eyes and did some abdominal breathing exercises.

"This is my routine," I said. "Otherwise, I don't feel sexy."

"I expected more drugs. And more junkie whores."

"It's still early in the day."

"Don't think you can joke your way out of this."

I opened an eye. "Why are you here? Why do you want to expose yourself—so to speak—to this world that you hate so much?"

"I want to understand what my son was thinking."

"He probably wanted to have sex with beautiful women. Most people can't. Like you. No offense. I'm guessing you can't sleep with, like, thirty different good-looking women, over a hundred times a year. Porn isn't calculus."

"I didn't even know he had sex. He never had a girlfriend."

"Then you didn't know your son as well as you thought you did," I said. "My dad doesn't know me at all. It happens. No use dwelling on it." I realized how bitter I sounded, how insensitive I was to his loss. "I'm not going to tell you how to mourn your son's death," I added.

"I could have done more," Tommy's father said, his eyes filling. "He didn't like going to church. He stopped talking to me because I made him go. Maybe I shouldn't have been so strict."

"Don't be so hard on yourself," I said. "What happened was a tragedy. The guy went nuts and your son was in the wrong place at the wrong time. I can't imagine what you're going through. There's nothing you could have done to stop it."

"What I keep coming back to is that he met you." He unlatched the cylinder on the revolver, fished single bullets out of a cargo pocket, and began loading the weapon.

No breathing exercise was going to help now. I envisioned my guts splattered all over the dressing room, and my dad, whom I hadn't spoken to in at least a decade, telling my mom with a shrug, "I told you something like that would happen."

A knock on the door. I opened it a crack. Mack's assistant, Cherry. She handed me the release form on a clipboard. I signed and returned it.

"Mack said to give you the thirty-minute warning."

"Thanks," I said, shutting the door. I reached into my dresser drawer for my emergency pills. I turned up the lights to view the expiration date. Still good. I popped one with a swig of water.

"If I could turn back time and make it so that I never met him, I would," I told Tommy's dad. "Is that what you want to hear?"

"Is she a performer?" he asked, nodding at the door.

"Cherry? She wants to be. If she toned up a little and maybe cleaned up the complexion, she could be making good money already."

"She looks barely eighteen."

"Clock's ticking. Once she gets started, she's going to look thirty in like six months, and then there will be another hundred eighteen-year-olds ready to take her spot."

"How do you live with yourself?"

"By cashing the checks."

"If I killed you right now, would anyone miss you?"

Maybe a few. I tried not to keep too many close friends. My mom still loved me, I thought. My fans might miss me. But what were they going to do? Hold a candlelight vigil for their favorite porn actor? Laud my contributions to the cum-munity? I'd long thought of myself as a service provider, except the service provided wasn't necessarily a net positive for society.

The sword murder-suicide was a crime felt throughout the industry. Some houses started hiring additional set security. Others required applications and background checks for every last person near a porn star. Too bad no one thought of a way to stop a crazy from showing up in my driveway.

"What does your father think of what you do?"

When I told him what I was doing for work after high school, I was driving him home from his food truck. He worked that truck by the airport for thirty years so that I could do whatever I dreamed would make me happy in life. He didn't expect porn to be on that list; hard to blame him, really, for the way he reacted. He clubbed my ear while we were on the I-10 East and said he would never speak to me again if I kept doing porn. He claimed he had never seen pornography in his life. He claimed he never masturbated. My honesty triggered a spew of his dishonesty.

"You think I'm the criminal here?" I said. "You think that just because you think what I do is a sin that I'm in the wrong? You're the one with the gun."

"Why would my son be so stupid to want to be like you?" he said. "I look at you and I see an uneducated person. I see someone who goes to the gym all the time but never studied in school. I see someone who has no family and lives in a big house counting his money. I see someone lying to himself that he's happy with his pathetic life."

"And who the fuck are you? What have *you* done other than spawn some loser-ass mope?"

"At least I'm honest," he said. "I have nothing left. My only son is gone. My wife has left me. I have nothing."

We seethed in silence. I anticipated the next door knock, my call to go to work. This was going to be the least pleasurable scene ever.

"You're one of the first," he said.

Media always asked about that. I didn't like talking about it. I was one of the few Asian male stars in the American industry.

I got my start because there was a demand for AMWF (Asian Male White Female) in Asian countries. A lot of my early work featured me fucking while my face and wang were blurred to get through the Japanese censors. The Japanese also really liked their rape, so I had to pretend to strangle girls while they fake-cried and screamed as I was inside them. Awful work. Worst of all, I'd only get paid $200-300 per scene! A dark period in my career.

Then *The Legend of Jon Bamboo* happened, and I took off. People actually wanted to see me fuck in America. And I did enough movies and met enough stars that they wanted to work with me. They knew I'd fuck them respectfully. I'd made enough money so I could say no to the BDSM and rape fantasy stuff. When you're nineteen or twenty, you can sort of fake your way through that shit. You can stay hard forever. Not so easy when you're thirty-five.

In summary, I wasn't James Deen or Johnny Sins, but Jon Bamboo was doing pretty well for himself.

Tommy's dad stepped up to me until our noses were almost touching. "What if you're one of the last? Then no one would want to be like you anymore."

I realized I wasn't afraid. I had achieved what I'd set out to achieve and everything that had come since was extra. And yes, I was a little disappointed. I grew up wanting to be Peter North, but now I knew that I could never be Peter North or Johnny Sins or James Deen. I could only be one of the Asian guys. I had my small moment in the sun and that was it. I'd succeeded, but at the same time, I'd failed. Sure, I couldn't enjoy some things because of the career I'd chosen: a relationship with my family, a normal love life. But I did the best I could with what God gave me.

"If you're going to kill me, just do it."

"Aren't you ashamed of who you are?" Tommy's father said. "You do the BTSM. You choke and hit women."

"BDSM," I corrected. "And I lightly slap and fake-choke. Nothing more. It's all consensual."

"You spit on them."

"How much did you enjoy your research? Did you jerk off to it?"

The mouth of the gun kissed my forehead. And then finally, the knock on the door.

"We're ready, Jon." Sindee Vuitton, one of my good friends in the industry. She came up around the same time, and we'd filmed lots of scenes together. We dated for a year. When she started, she skyrocketed to fame as a barely legal. Now, ten years later, she was twenty-nine and a MILF. Sometimes they even asked her to do Mature. On a normal day, I never had trouble keeping it hard for her. Her husband is a chef, nice guy—we played golf sometimes. Her three-year-old son was super cute.

"Come on in, Sin," I said. Tommy's father wheeled his weapon behind his back.

"Are you okay?" she said, peeking in. "I heard you needed thirty minutes."

"I didn't take it," I lied. "Come in. Meet my dad."

"Oh hi!" Sindee said, shaking the gunman's free hand. "Pleasure to meet you, Mr. Bamboo."

"He likes the bondage porn," I said.

Sindee's eyes widened.

"It's a Japanese thing," I added.

She smiled, smacking me on the arm. That was our inside joke. It took her about five years of working together for her to remember what kind of Asian I was.

"What the hell are you doing here?" Sindee said to me. "Go out with your dad. We could have rescheduled."

"I came to see you," I said, locking eyes, hoping she'd see that something was wrong. "So what do you do?" she asked Tommy's dad, missing my unspoken message.

"I'm a postal worker."

"Of course he is," I blurted.

He glared at me.

"Why don't you stay here, Pops? I'm not sure you should actually see what I do."

"Oh, I do," he said. "I want the full BTS. I love the behind-the-scenes videos."

Sindee laughed. "Your dad *is* a perv."

Even with Sindee, the scene was a struggle. Took over an hour. My erection lasted too long, and I couldn't finish. She looked distracted; I looked distracted. Mack kept asking if I was okay. Everyone kept asking if I was okay. I wasn't fucking okay. Fucking okay was standing over there in the corner, watching me, waiting to blow my brains out.

Afterward, downstairs in the kitchen, a robed Sindee took my sweat-soaked self aside. "I'm sorry I touched your hair," she said. "I know you don't like that."

I hadn't even noticed.

"You must be so sore," Sindee said.

"You too," I said, shaking my head. "I'm sorry."

"Don't be. You know you can always talk to me, right?"

I checked over my shoulder to see where my tormentor was. Mack was showing him our dungeon set and complaining that my inability to cum caused him to be behind schedule. I pulled Sindee close and muttered: "He's not my dad. He's Tommy Kok's dad. He's got a gun. He thinks I got his son killed."

Sindee smiled and nodded as she eyed Herbert's father. "Fuck," she whispered.

"Son!" Tommy's father shouted from the dungeon.

"Dad?" I looked for sharp objects. Nothing but cheese knives. "Let's go get some lunch."

"I'm not hungry," he said, walking over.

"I need some food before my next shoot," I said. "And I need to shower." I hugged Sindee goodbye. "Call the police," I whispered in her ear.

"I think Sindee should have lunch with us," Tommy's father said. "I'd love to talk to your friend."

And so there we were, in my dressing room again, waiting for burritos to be delivered from El Pollo Loco. Behind closed doors, I told Tommy's father that Sindee knew who he was.

"So it looks like you'll have to commit a double murder today," I said.

"You should know, Mr. Kok," Sindee said, "that Jon had nothing to do with your son's murder."

"Shut the fuck up and sit the fuck down, whore!"

"Don't talk to her that way," I said. "Is that the type of Christian language you use to speak to women?"

"Women do what men say in my church."

"So church is just like porn."

"You corrupted my son!"

"You didn't support him! You think that just because you feed a kid and send him to school that that makes you a father? No. You have to support what will make your son happy. When he was old enough, he'd learn all on his own that the world is shit. He didn't need you to tell him too. All you had to do was say: go be happy. I love you and I'm proud of you. Did you ever say that? I bet you didn't. My dad didn't."

"Stop it!" Sindee cried out. "Both of you. How is this going to help, Mr. Kok? We can't bring your son back."

And that was when Tommy's dad crumpled on the futon and began to weep. He rested the gun on the dresser and covered his face with both hands. He began to release clenched sobs.

Sindee sat next to Mr. Lin as he cried. I felt bad for him and racked my brain for more memories with Tommy that I could share. He said he hated college. He was glad to be away from home so he could meet women. He flunked out of freshman year. His story was a lot like mine. That's why I kept talking to him. That's why I gave him an in. I couldn't say that I made the right choices. All I could say was that they worked out. Tommy made me feel better about those choices.

"He wished he didn't have to choose between you and himself," I said. "He told me this. In my suite. While we looked over the Bellagio fountains. He was a good person. I could tell."

Mr. Lin was in full-on ugly-cry-face mode now. I'm not 100% sure that was a real memory of Tommy. It seemed like something he might say. We did look out over the Bellagio fountains at the AVN awards that year. At least that part was true.

The doorknob started rattling and Mack and Cherry asked what was going on. Sindee and I locked eyes and an understanding passed between us. I swiped the gun and stuffed it in the dresser while she unlocked the door, letting Mack and Cherry in. Before Mr. Lin realized what was happening, I threw myself onto him. Something in the futon frame snapped and it folded flat under our weights, and I held Mr. Lin's arms down against the mattress. He was just a frail old man who didn't weigh much more than the women I worked with. I waited for him to stop struggling. I was sitting on his chest like I was the girl on top, and Mack was holding up one of his dungeon paddles, ready to use it. The El Pollo Loco delivery guy appeared in the doorway with our burritos.

How did one even begin to explain a morning like this?

I drove Mr. Lin home. A real memory of Tommy in Las Vegas returned. "He said you always wanted to own a restaurant, but you could never get the funds together. He said you were a good cook."

For the first time that day, Mr. Lin smiled. Sheepishly so. "Then we had Herbert," he said, his voice phlegmatic.

When I dropped him off in front of his house in San Gabriel, he got out of the car, looked at me, his lower lip trembling.

"Thank you for telling my boy what he wanted to hear," he said.

SILENCE, FATHER

delvon t. mattingly

When Grandmother passed away, Father grew reticent. And I was okay with it, since he abandoned his routine of scolding me for lacking masculinity. Since he stopped tickling me and calling me girl-crazy if I laughed. Since he didn't condemn every tear that fell from my face, spewing the same toxic rhetoric of how I needed to emotionally withdraw and appear similar to a parapet wrapped in black derma, to protect everyone around me, just like him. When I thought I would cry most, I felt nothing.

Weeks passed, and he still hadn't spoken. He didn't leave his bedroom unless to cook or work. His girlfriend advised me to console him, but I had no idea what that meant. "He needs someone to be there for him, a source of solace," she stressed.

I reasoned, *Shouldn't that be you too? There's no way he's saddened. If anything, he's angry, afraid of exacerbating the latter sentiment.*

Regardless, I entered the room. The eye cascades were imminent, a lump in my throat burgeoning with every passing second. I saw grandmother harboring the space around him. With only her spectral eyes, she engaged in combat with the monstrosity inside me, the entity nurtured to siphon all liquids from my pores. Sweat. Tears. Blood. Nothing could escape without censure.

My body felt empty, but not like before. The internal entity existed out of fear, and when it vanished, I comfortably sat upright on the bed next to father. I had almost forgotten about crying until I beheld his glossy eyes. He sustained an image of an emotional bulwark for nearly a decade, only for it to crumble due to sorrow. Witnessing this was brutal. I had to turn away.

We held our gazes forward. All I remember was thinking, *I'm not allowed to let you see me like this.* Without looking, I placed my hand on his shoulder only to feel damp blotches on his shirt. Then I broke, both of us equally invested in our assured grief. Grandmother enfolding us in a space imbued with silence.

ANIMALS MAUL ME

by rebekah morgan

Sometimes I don't know what to say. Sometimes I don't know how to save my own faggotass from heartbreak. Sometimes the trees catch on fire and we burn furniture and listen to bluegrass and we talk about butterbeans and we cry and cry and cry. Sometimes my friends lose their homes and sometimes I can okra and green tomatoes with fresh garlic.

Everything is covered in mud from my bibs to my dog to my boots to my bedspread. I spent the summer draggin my own heart through the mud and most of the fall and the winter too. But, it's been worth it for the most part. When you find something good you have to hold onto it with all the strength the mountains provide you with.

Sometimes you can watch hearts break in public if you know what you're lookin' at. I saw a boy eat spaghetti. He ate like a tiger, like a toad, like a firefly. His eyes bulged out of his head and he held his fork so delicately, it was as if he was scared it might break. I watched him as he slowly spun the spaghetti against the cresting lip of the plate. I heard the boy talk to the spaghetti. The boy said " I would hate me too, if I were you" and the boy said to the spaghetti, "let's pretend that this is all new, all fresh, that nothing bad has ever happened, that we are meeting just now for the first time." After a while the boy wiped his face with a cloth napkin and then the spaghetti was gone. The boy sat at the table for a long time running his finger around the rim of his plate. The boy picked up his fork and inspected it and placed it back down on the plate. The boy picked up a knife off of the table that had gone unused during the meal and stuck it in his shirt pocket with the butter blade pointing down. I heard the boy say "I miss you" and take a sip of water from a tall glass on the table. I heard the boy say "you're not forgotten" and he got up to clear his plate.

Call it heartbreak on the hillside or call it vulnerability. Today I smudged my bedroom with sage I stole from my ex-hippie roommate. I smudged the rattan chair with my Romanian rug thrown over the back and the sheepskin draped over the arm, I smudged the dog bowl filled with freezing brown well water, I smudged my shotgun patiently waiting in the corner of my room with the safety off. When my friends come over they're always surprised by the delicate nature of my bedroom.

Animals maul my flesh and I find comfort in that somehow. It's like putting a cigarette out on your arm after your sugarpie leaves you for good, but better somehow. Animals maul me and I don't care.

If a wild hog rolled up bedside and asked me to jab its tusk straight through my cheek, I'd probably oblige. There's so much fever inside of me and so much ice held back behind my eyes. The fever fights the ice, but no one ever wins. Small lizards wedge themselves in my armpits and bite me as hard as they can without ever drawing blood.

I tell myself I don't care what the animals have to say about me but also, I care more than anything about it. I care about it in a way that makes me sick, worrying about fairness and divided time and whether or not I can still cry. I don't want to be told not to cry while I stand in a shallow grave trying my best to grow a mustache.

I wanna talk to dragonflies about their dreams and ask what makes them sad and ask the dragonflies how they think I can be a better man. I looked into a mirror and all I saw was the white thickness of a cow's skull floating midair. Its hollowed eyes staring back at me as if to say, "You too are empty." I looked at the skull and I said "introduce me to the maggots who ate your head." I looked at the skull and I said "so much salt within you and you still just wind up dead."

I've kissed everything around me and every animal that's ever come to me. I've kissed the stones and the river and the trees overgrown, the turtle doves and the armadillos, the flying fish and the parakeets too. I've kissed everything around me in a way that made things grow inside me, for at least a little while.

PINBALL & PDA

misty skaggs

My boyfriend, he doesn't dig on public displays of affection. I'd say he doesn't want to bring undo attention to himself, except he weighs four hundred pounds and sports a fourteen-inch mohawk. Takes me forty-five minutes and two packs of Knox to cement the atomic orange shock of hair before we head out of our piece-of-shit trailer in his piece-of-shit Cadillac, burning down JJ, dusting the cornfields with exhaust. We're flying towards town, towards the smokey buzz of the bar. The scene is as unfamiliar to me as the flat, beige landscape. The social politics go far beyond my grasp. I was a teenage bumpkin when I ran away from cushy college life to shack up with an amateur bass player. And his mom. I'm twenty-one and I've spent the past two years discovering I can hold my liquor. Even way out in the dead middle of the Midwest, I upturn and then cultivate alcoholic roots that coil and snake back to the hills of Appalachia where I was born. He drives and I drink and I hide it from him in a big gulp cup half full of orange soda. I chomp my fruit-stripe-and- vodka-flavored gum and man the sound system, weaving a perfect driving mix from a stack of scratched cd's, a sound track to cover our shameful silence. I've taken up sleeping on the couch. At least we're into the same bands.

Me, I like to hang on my man. Press my weight hot and heaving into his bulk. Especially when the lights are dim and the music is thumping through my thick thighs and PBR's are two for a dollar. But he brushes me off. Swats me away like a fly. I dressed up tonight, plump flesh pressed into fishnet stockings like a juicy, punk rock ham. Fresh from Kentucky. My boyfriend says he thinks the pink Converse I'm wearing are "cute." No comment on my legs, propped up on the cracked vinyl dashboard.

"Too bad you can't play pinball in that shirt," he says.

My boyfriend doesn't even chance a glance at my heavy, milky tits stuffed into a studded push-up bra with the straps reflecting headlights. His tattooed hands gripped the wheel firmly at ten and two, watching the long grey stretch of asphalt roll out in front of us. My green eyes roll and I stretch and I wave at the trucker above me, leering down at me from the fast lane. My boyfriend is a sore fucking loser. He doesn't like the surprising way my nimble little sausage fingers fly over the paddles. He prefers me in a t-shirt and jeans. He won't kiss me tonight. Shoving me into the pit passes for copping a feel in our relationship.

My boyfriend will spend most of the night schmoozing with hipster assholes in the blind hope of forging the perfect band. And I won't talk to anyone but the bartender. All I can hear is the thump of the beat and the foamy chug of my bottle. All I can hope for are sweat-soaked boozy bodies brushing up against mine. The bubble gum whine in the air makes me bounce and I forget. Forget that in a few hours I'll fall asleep unsatisfied, sad and drunk. Crying for the want of gravy and biscuits for breakfast. My boyfriend won't notice.

Like he doesn't notice me picking my way through the crowd to the pinball machine, in spite of my skimpy new top. Like he doesn't see the way I jiggle and tilt. Once I've had my fill and my multi-ball, I give the free game to the bartender and take a free drink from a skinny, Sid Vicious wanna be in an uniform dirty white wife-beater and leather jacket.

"Is that guy you came in with, like, your brother or something?" the stranger asks.

We sit too close together in a back booth and I feel his bony, foreign fingers exploring, finding the hole ripped in my panty hose after a long night. His thumb jerks toward the silhouette of my soon-to-be-ex-boyfriend.

"Something like that," I decide. I wrap my lips around a beer bottle and make up my mind to be drinking bourbon by this time next week.

BASS

ashleigh bryant phillips

I know I can get better if I want to. Everybody can get better if they want to.

At the Duck Thru the black ladies are talking 'bout the Bradley man that used to be sheriff in Halifax County. He killed himself yesterday. Melissa's rescue squad was called out to it. They say he called 911 and told them he was having chest pains. And by the time Melissa and them got there he'd shot himself in the chest with his sawed off twelve gauge. He was still alive when they found him. Wallowing right there in his recliner. Melissa said he'd sold everything in the house except for that recliner. Like he'd been getting ready for it for months.

The black ladies are making sausage biscuits. And all Krystal's doing is looking at me.

"Right wet out there ain't it, Donnie?" she says.

I nod and rain falls off the end of my hat.

She giggles and leans on the counter, pushes her breasts together.

I ask her for a can of Grizzly, and she bends over like she's stretching. And I wonder for minute what she'd be like, how she likes it. Me taking her from behind. Wrapping that white blond hair round my hand one good time. And it's alright. She's been acting like she wants me to be thinking about it— going on a while now. Since she turned up at our church, bringing them kids to Vacation Bible School.

She puts the can on the counter and says, "I won't tell Melissa." Melissa put me on the prayer list Sunday. Her cousin just got mouth cancer so she thinks I will too.

Krystal clicks her fingernails on the lighter case, her pointer finger has a little diamond in it. "Just got 'em done yesterday. You like 'em?" She holds out her hands in front of me, wiggles her fingers.

Before I can answer she turns to them ladies, smiles at them and says, "Miss Gretchen and Hilly think they're gaudy."

"But anyways." She turns back to me and bangs the register with her fist to open it. She hands me my change, her bracelets clinking. "You got a plumbing snake? Melissa said she thought y'all did. I think one of my boys done put a truck in the commode."

"Don't worry 'bout it," I say. If I don't help Krystal, I'll hear it from Melissa so I tell Krystal I'll come over 'round five.

Krystal tells me to call her before I head over. She writes her number on the back of my receipt. I put it in my pocket without looking at it.

When I walk out the door them women are trying to figure if the Bradley man is gonna have an open casket.

"If he don't look too bad, then they ought to do it," one of 'em says.

"It's the right thing to do… for the family," says the other one.

I sit in the truck some and watch the cars fly down Highway 258. Flinging puddles out the road. Fore I even went out to the MacDaniel farm this morning, I knew it was gonna be a swamp. All that corn won't be worth five cents. Count of that tropical depression, rain's been here all week. I can't do nothing. But I called Wayne anyway like a damn piece of shit cause me and Melissa need the money now with another baby coming. I called him and asked him did he want me to do anything out there on the MacDaniel farm. If there was any work I could do on that old picker in his shop. Wayne said he wished he could help me, but he'll have me back in the field once the rain lets up. He tells me to tell Melissa he said, "Hello." And right now she's rubbing her belly so happy.

And right now I'm sitting here alone outside the Duck Thru in my truck and one thing I can always do right is count the teeth on this Grizzly can. That bear comes out having five teeth every time you count it. I put in a good dip. Hell, when me and Melissa was youngins she'd dip too. Don't know if she really enjoyed it, or if she was just trying to show off to all us on the baseball team. But she'd put a dip in bigger than anything you'd seen and sit right there on the tailgate looking just as pretty as you please, swinging her legs, telling us how she loved the tingle of it.

Now she's bought them special vitamins for having healthy babies. It's the first thing she does every morning. Takes that bottle from her nightstand and pops them vitamins and looks at me and grins.

It didn't even feel like nothing when I made that baby with her. I thought that it would feel different but it just felt like every other time.

If I sit here too long folks'll see me sitting here. Don't want anybody to think anything. I just want something to happen. Or get caught up in something until something does. Wish I could just go to sleep and wake up and feel like there's something to look forward to.

I get out the truck and dig through all the shit in the truck bed. I find my cane pole and cooler and figure I'll go out to the pond. Long as I know my family's been fishing in this pond back off behind Slade Store Road. It's real nice, lots of pin oaks and gumball tress round the edges. A big Magnolia so old the roots rise up out of the ground and you can sit there on em. Don't nobody ever come out there. Nobody to look at, nobody to look at me.

Daddy always said there was a bass out there but I ain't never seen one. Pond's too small for a bass. My daddy worked for Wayne's daddy. That's how that works. Won't until I was grown that I that I realized Daddy half assed everything Hell he half parred everything. He always told me he learned everything he knew from his daddy. I never knew the old man, he died before I was born. But I heard my daddy's old man hollered at him from the time my daddy was a baby. Scared Daddy so much he didn't talk until he was five years old.

Reckon that's why my daddy did some things to me too. I tell Melissa sometimes at night before we sleep and she listens and tells me it's alright. Melissa's too good a woman for me.

Soon as I pull down in there, I spit out my dip and I find the Rich and Rare in my glovebox. It's the best Canadian whiskey that's bang for your buck. I drink till the rain lets up to a drizzle and it feels like time is moving easier. And the rain looks like static on the pond. I get out and catch some crickets easy. I catch me a couple baby brim with the crickets, and bait the brim for a damn bass. I throw in round the edges and start jigging the line. A bass would be something.

Truth is before our baby came I came out here and swam out to the middle of that water. Went right in with my boots on. I wanted the water to fill me up till there won't nothing left. I wanted something to come and just pull me to the bottom. But I just floated there all afternoon watched the sky change to stars. I was waiting there when I heard Melissa calling for me. I watched the light she was shining on the water, watched it get closer to me. She was screaming my name, running down into the water with her big belly, pulling me out. Telling me she loved me over and over and I couldn't say nothing. She was pulling stuff out of my hair and beard. Then she stopped and showed me. "Look, forsythia blooms," she said.

The line tugs and then pulls hard like a snatch and I know, I can feel it. It's a bass. And he's fighting too boy. I get him to where I can see his eyes and get him on the shore. His stripe is pretty and straight. He's got to be about eight pounds.

I lay him in the tall grass, watch his gills open and close. He moves his fins real pretty. And he's bleeding from where he swallowed the hook. And looking at him like that, I almost don't want to keep him. But I sit there and watch his mouth move till the blood stops coming out of him. And I can't hardly believe it all. My fucking daddy.

I fill the cooler up with water and put him down in it easy.

My watch says quarter till 4. But I figure I'll call Krystal up anyway, get on over there a little early. And I don't know how she did it, but the way Krystal curled the "y" on her name looks like a damn heart, like some bullshit. I know she lives in Arrowhead but don't know which trailer is hers. I call her up and she tells me she lives at the back edge in the blue singlewide. The one with the baby pool she says.

Only time I ever been out to Arrowhead was when Wayne's son asked me to bring him out here to buy some drugs from Big Bay Odom. I pass Big Bay's trailer and him and all them are sitting out in their yard watching me, smoking with their shirts off. When I pull up to Krystal's all these cats go running out from everywhere. And all her kids are watching me from the window, all those little heads, one on top of the other.

I grab the plumbing snake out the truck bed. And I check on the bass and his gills are still opening and closing. He'll probably be dead by the time I look at him again, suffocate in that water. I put in another dip and I hear

Krystal yell at the kids. She flings open the front door and hollers, "Don't be a stranger Donnie, come on in the house." She's in a top she's about to fall out of. I know then what all this is gonna be. I look back towards Big Bay Odom's. They're still watching me. I can feel them watching me when I step into Krystal's trailer. She hugs me and thanks me for coming over and her kids all go stand in front of the couch. There's four of them, a boy 'bout twelve, two middle ones, and a baby. They all have white blonde hair like her. The place smells like cat piss.

"Y'all 'member Mr. Donnie don't ya?" She tugs at her shirt to show more of her breasts. "He's the one that cuts the grass at church."

The middle girl starts to pick her nose.

Krystal pops her hand.

"What's that?" The oldest points to the plumbing snake in my hand.

"A plumbing snake, ain't that a funny name?" Krystal says.

"Don't look like a snake to me," the middle girl says.

They giggle and she tells them to go play in their room. The oldest one looks back at me and follows the rest of them ripping down the hall. Krystal leads me to her room and hollers to them to make her some more pictures. And I look back at the fridge and it's already covered in paper, every one of them is pictures of horses. Horses running in fields, on the beach with big suns over them. She'll have to take some down to make room for more.

Krystal's bed is made up with velvet looking pillows that say "Angel." She picks one up and squeezes it against her. Her skin looks glittery. "Got these from the Dollar General," she says, "Can you believe it? They're getting more cosmopolitan all the time."

"Yeah," I say, "Where you want me to put this plumbing snake?"

"That sink there's fine," she points behind me to her bathroom.

There's a big picture of Marilyn Monroe blowing a kiss above the commode and Krystal's got a candle lit in front of the bathroom mirror, smells like cotton candy. It's next to a pink ashtray slam full of butts. It's a glass one, looks antique. I tell her that most folks think you need a plumbing snake when they just need a plunger.

"Well I tried the plunger already. All day yesterday I was trying that plunger." She comes into the bathroom and lights a Virginia Slim with a flowery lighter. She edges up on the counter and sits her lighter by the candle.

"I've been having to use the kid's bathroom," she says, "And with all of them, it's right crowded." She flicks her cigarette into the ashtray. "Bout like living in the old days," she laughs.

"I reckon," I say.

I grab the plunger from behind the commode and while I'm plunging, I can see her out the corner of my eye tracing her knees with her diamond fingernail. I can feel whatever that's in the commode give and I spit my dip out in it. I give it a flush and it unclogs just fine.

"Well, that won't much of nothing," she says and she stubs out her cigarette.

"I don't think it was a toy, coulda just been a lot of paper," I say.

She gets down off the counter and wiggles her toes into the pink rug. "I knew it, I've been telling Jeenie to stop using so much paper, but she likes using my bathroom. What can I tell her? She's my only girl."

Krystal is acting dumb but she knows what she's doing. I study her feet. She's picked every one of her toenails down into the quick. There's dried blood in the corners of some of 'em.

"You just don't know how much I appreciate it," she says. She comes closer. "It's hard here you know. I need all the help I can get." She runs her fingers down my shirt buttons. Her nails make a sound when they touch my buttons. Like a clink like a tap… "And I know you need some help too sometimes.

"Let me make you feel better, Donnie."

And she puts a finger into my shirt between the buttons, scratches my chest. "I know you've been hurting," she says, "for a long time."

And I'm caught up in it. I don't have no control. I pick her up and put her on the counter and rake my teeth down her neck, all the way down to her collarbone. Her nails go into my shoulders and her heels go into my ass. I shove my hand under her bra and her breasts are hot and soft at the same time. I bite her nipples and she clinches harder, gasps.

"You like it hard, don't you." Krystal says.

I throw her on the bed. She gets up to reach for me and I pull her legs out from under her. She gets up again and I grab her hair, wrap it 'round my hand one good time.

"You're a bad man, Donnie Dunlow," she says.

I stand there and hold her out from me on the bed and she likes that. She's making good noise. I want to feel her shaking while I'm inside her. So hard inside her.

"That's right, I am a bad man," I tell her.

She's trying to reach for me, clawing for me like it's all she knows how to do.

"Fuck me, Donnie," she gets louder, "I said I want you to FUCK me."

A kid starts screaming, comes flying down the hall. And the bedroom door starts beating, the doorknob shaking, turning so fast.

I let go of Krystal's hair and she falls on the bed. The bathroom light makes my shadow on her. She turns over to face me and I see now all of her naked body. Her chest heaves, her legs stretch.

"I'll be there in a minute, Baby," she yells to the door. She starts to get up and stops in front of me, looks at me like she's about to cry.

I'm back where I started and I can see everything now for what it is. And all I can do is slap her. I slap the shit out of her, slap her as hard as I can.

I pick her hair out from 'round my fingers and watch the beating door. When I open it the middle girl's standing under me wringing her hands.

"Tell them to stop chasing me with that spider," she points down the hall.

They're all looking at me from the end of the hall. But I still wipe my face and pull myself together. And I tell them I gotta bass in the back of my truck.

Heading out the trailer the cats come up underneath my feet, bout to damn trip me. The baby runs straight into the baby pool fast as lightning, even with all the rain it still looks like the water's been standing in it for months. The middle girl grabs him, wipes the green shit off his fat little legs. The boys crawl up the sides and lean in over the truck bed. I open up the cooler, and he don't look the same anymore. He don't look as beautiful. He's starting to die.

"Now that there is the prettiest bass I've ever seen!" The oldest takes a picture of him on his phone. "You'll have to take me with you next time, man."

One of the cats jump in the truck bed, looks like it's got a stomach full of worms. The oldest boy picks it up and starts scratching it's head.

"Lookee!" The girl holds up the baby and the baby sticks it's head in the cooler.

The bass moves his tail fin and barely makes the water slosh. The cat perks up. The baby squeals. It's right pitiful.

"What you gon' do with him, Mithter Donnie?" The middle boy has a lisp. "He's so big, he'd liable to take up the whole wall!" He holds his hands out real wide above his head and the rest of them laugh.

I look out towards Halifax County and it looks like another storm cloud is coming. It'll be raining again soon. I tell the kids to head back in the house. And Big Bay Odom and all the trash sitting in their front yards, smoking cigarettes in Arrowhead, sees me leave out of there.

I sit in the truck outside my house and I tell myself that I caught a bass and that my wife will be happy. And that I am a good man coming home to my family. I am a good man.

When I walk in the house, first thing Melissa says to me is, "Where's the diapers?"

She hits the side of the skillet with the spoon and puts her other hand on her hip, "I told you this morning 'fore you went out that Bailey needs some more diapers."

Bailey's on the floor reaching for her Mama with cheerios stuck to her chest.

I grab Melissa and kiss her on the mouth.

"Golly, honey," she says, "What's gotten into you?"

I tell her to close her eyes. I watch her a little there with her eyes closed wiping her hands on a dish rag. "Did you get them pork chops like I asked," she pushes a curl out her face.

I run and grab the bass out of the cooler and the baby laughs at me when I come in. And when I tell Melissa to open her eyes she is so happy. She says how special the bass is. She tells the baby her Daddy ought to go in the paper for a bass like this. I'm standing there in the kitchen holding it and I be damn if he ain't dead yet. His gills open and close so slow. Melissa don't even notice. She's kissing me, taking off my cap. She's taking a picture of me and him on her phone.

"I'll caption it: MY GREATEST CATCH," she says. She giggles at her own joke. She looks at me like she loves me.

"Let me put him down," I tell her. I put him on the cutting board and he lays there real still. We stand over him together and I put my hands around her waist.

"He's so pretty Donnie," she says. "You ought to mount him. We could put him above the TV!"

I watch him stop moving.

Melissa moves my hand to be on her belly. "We could mount him and put him in our little man's room," she says it so sweet like.

But I don't want to think about that. I tell her let's eat him. He'll be good and nice with all the vitamins and all that stuff our babies need. I can't believe how happy I sound saying it. And I rub her belly and she puts her hands on mine.

Melissa says that she'll clean him, that she'll finish taking care of supper. She tells me I deserve it. I pour a glass of tea and I sit on the couch and look at the baby in front of the TV. Melissa keeps going on about the bass.

I scratch my beard and some glitter falls outta it. What did Krystal say to those youngins when they all jumped in front of each other showing her the horses they made for her? I don't remember. I watch the ice melt in my glass, watch the glass drip on the outside. It's gonna make a ring on the end table. I feel like the glitter is all over me. I feel like it's shining all over me. Then Melissa hollers for me.

She's standing there with blood on her hands.

"I can't do it," she says, "you're gonna have to get the head. His bones are too strong."

When I bring the knife down it feels like the rest of his body jerks. His backbone is so strong I have to really work at it until it breaks in two. Krystal said she knew I'd been hurting. I 'bout can't stand it.

Melissa puts her hand on my shoulder and then puts his head in a bowl in the sink.

And I go take a shower and get all the glitter and blood and everything off of me.

When Melissa says the blessing, she opens her eyes to me and rubs her belly.

"He just kicked," she says, "He's so excited about his Daddy's bass."

I know damn well that's not true. She's not even showing yet. But I feel excited that she feels excited. And that makes me feel like it's something I can smile about.

Melissa fried the bass perfect. And she eats him like she's starving, like she's been waiting for him all along. It makes me feel good. In between mouthfuls she asks me what work Wayne had for me today, and I tell her nothing.

"Didn't even have nothing at the shop?" she says.

I shake my head and the baby bangs her hands in carrot shit in the highchair. She's even picking at half a filet.

"Well, y'all will be out in the field soon enough." Melissa wipes the baby's face and hands. "Weatherman says this rain will be easing off soon."

I take my first bite and he don't taste musty or anything, cleanest fish I've ever tasted.

"What about Krystal," Melissa says. "You get up with her?"

"Well, yeah," I say.

"You didn't charge her nothing did you?" Melissa says. "You know she can't barely afford any shoes for those kids."

I try to remember if those kids had any shoes on.

"I told the women's auxiliary that we need to take up a love offering for 'em." Melissa talks to the baby getting her out of the highchair. "Ain't that right, sweet baby girl?"

"And you know what," she stops on her way from the table, "I'll put some of them filets together and you can take them to her tomorrow. We've got enough to feed an army."

I think of Krystal poking my bass apart with her fingernails, feeding all those youngins like little birds. Them underneath each side of her reaching up with their open mouths.

"You're a good woman, Melissa," I say.

I clean off the table. And then I get the rest of my bass out the sink. I take him out and dump him at the edge of the yard.

Bailey sleeps in our bed between us. She don't move or wake up for nothing. Melissa thinks it's sweet.

Melissa puts her Bible down on her stomach and I can tell she's praying, praying for everybody, but I know she's praying for me. I've known that since she found me out there in the pond. And I know she wants to tell me that she knows that's where I caught that bass. But she won't say it because she don't want to hurt me.

"Don't forget the Bradley man's wake is tomorrow," she says.

I think about that Bradley man sitting alone in his recliner, alone in his empty house, in the middle of the afternoon. He probably had the blinds pulled. But he didn't want to be there for days until someone found him. Have his children come in and find him like that. That's why he called the rescue squad.

"Did he say anything when y'all got there?" I say, "I mean, was he able to talk?"

"Honey, I don't want to remember." She brushes my hair of my forehead and starts to touch my face.

"Well a man that kills himself ain't a man at all," I say. I feel like that's important for me to say. That's what my daddy said when L.G. Cook found out he had cancer and shot himself down one of his paths. That was the first time I remember knowing about anything like that.

"I think I'm proud of you, Donnie Dunlow," she says.

I can't do nothing but turn over away from her.

She tells me she loves me.

I look out and watch the rain start to hit the window and I tell her I love her too.

Melissa's pager goes off at about 11:45. She kisses the baby and is gone. I turn on the scanner on the nightstand and listen to her. She says there's a bad wreck out on Galatia Church Road.

Way off I can hear the sirens. I get my Grizzly from under the dresser and I start to pack my dip, I slap it harder and harder. I put in my dip and look at my hands. I look at the back of them and I look at the front, I turn them over and over. I go to the gun cabinet and find half a bottle of Rich and Rare and sit it next to me. I spit out my dip and start to drink.

Melissa's still on the scanner. The baby's still asleep. And I sit and watch the rain start sideways, hear the lighting come. Next thing I know I near 'bout finish off the bottle.

I head out the house and it's so dark I can't see nothing. I walk into the push mower. It's already rusting, sinking in the mud. Every man ought to have a shed for his tools. But that don't matter now. The rain makes the bottle slip in my hands, but I drink it damn straight. Right there in my backyard, right there in front of the fields.

And don't you know that the damn coons and dogs came out in the storm and took the last parts of my bass. I'm down on my hands feeling for him. I want to find where I broke him in two.

TWO STORIES

kim magowan

Fitting

I love Rachel, but after fourteen years together and two children, sex isn't the same. Being inside her feels like inserting a finger in a nostril. Where I used to feel the grip of her, I'm aware of empty space. And none of my solutions work: sticking pillows under her, though Rachel claims she feels like she's the princess on the pea getting fucked atop a pile of mattresses. Doggie-style, her on top, it's all the same. I feel shrunken, as I literally am—according to my GP only 5'11" now, no longer six feet. And of course death looms, still decades away but within sight now, a cypress on the horizon.

No doubt these observations seem well-worn, just as my wife is well-worn, but I present them not as excuses but rather as context. Rachel and I fit well in so many ways, just not, unfortunately, in this most literal sense. There I find myself fitting better with a young, childless woman. In her late-twenties, Eileen is so pale she's almost amphibious. The blue veins networking her milky breasts make her look like some transparent creature, a jellyfish.

But to be inside her is to be clasped in the warm grip of life.

Outside of bed, we have only the blandest things to say to each other—conversation as stuttering and out-of-tune as my wonky record player—but who cares? I'm not looking for a partner in any sense other than this specific one. I see Eileen as an exceptionally graceful woman I ask to dance at a wedding: she has that little to do with Rachel, with my marriage.

Rachel and I are well-matched, in ways not necessarily forecastable in advance. For instance, our parenting is in accord. We are similarly delighted by and realistic about our children. Whereas Lillian, my ex-wife, is a deeply flawed mother, raising our daughter Annika to be an eye-rolling, gustily sighing teenager, with eyes for nothing but the small glow of her phone. After one exhausting visit from Annika, I complained to Rachel that Annika's mother was an odd mixture of neglectful and indulgent. "There should be a word for that combination," I said, and Rachel said, "There is: negligent."

But then Rachel proceeded to downplay Annika's obnoxiousness—"It's fucking hard to be sixteen." She's a good step-mother as well as mother, as well as wife. In so many fundamental categories, I am blessed to have my witty, clear-eyed Rachel, with the exception of this limited, inconsequential way in which we no longer fit.

And I have so convinced myself of Eileen's inconsequence—of her status as merely a dance partner at a wedding, that unthreatening—that I'm shocked to return from extracting leaves from our gutters to a transformed Rachel, red and puckered, like one of Caravaggio's vegetable-faced people. She shakes my phone at me: "Who the fuck is Eileen!?" On our bed she's put my roller bag. "So this is why you've been so cheerful lately. This is why I hear you singing in the shower," she says, in a voice both wet with tears and dry as grit. "Now it all fits."

Surfaces

At Jenna's, we have to be vigilant about every surface: we must not track dirt from the back yard into the kitchen (Jenna's is the only house I've ever seen with two doormats). Once when I put a glass down on the coffee table—this was the ordinary coffee table in the family room, not the fancy one in the living room—Jenna's mother came flying in with a coaster. She reminded me of a cartoon character running, legs a blurry wheel.

So I prefer hanging out at my house, where everything is dirty and no one gives a shit. No one's dad says, "So, Will, what colleges are you considering?"

Sometimes Jenna looks around my bedroom squeamishly, like there's no clean place to sit.

In two weeks her parents are taking her to New England to tour a bunch of colleges. They'll be gone ten days. "I'm going to miss you so much," Jenna tells me, as if she's going into combat, and will be gone for years. I tease her for being melodramatic, but I can't shake the feeling that when she leaves, she'll be gone for good.

My ex-girlfriend Amy-Rose said to me once, "You only like me because I'm pretty." She wasn't wrong, though I could've retorted, "You only like me because I play guitar and have a car." A shitty car, but still. Instead I said, "Man, you have such a huge ego." I gave her crap for one aspect of her comment (that she believed she was hot) rather than acknowledging the other (that the only valuable thing about Amy-Rose was her surface).

I lie on my bed watching Jenna look up college websites on her laptop. The buildings are gray or sandstone or oatmeal or brick, but all have the same swaths of ivy, like dudes of different ethnicities who all have the same facial hair. I didn't know the ivy thing was so literal. Over time, ivy damages stone. Watching Jenna click and scroll, I feel like something sticky that clings, for now, onto her skin.

LAVINA

eleanor levine

"Do you drive a car?" she asked on the way to Hyannis.

"No."

"Is it because you have a handicap?"

I had never passed my written test.

I also felt as estranged from driving a car as I did Stanley Kaplan's GRE prep course.

Lavina, while driving, explained where Hyannis was. She was perplexed by my inability to grasp the logic of her map.

"Did you also fail geography?" she asked. "Maybe you have a directional disability? Anyway, what do you do for a living?"

"I work at a prophylactics factory in the Bronx," I replied.

"Don't you want to do something more important?"

Lavina lived in a duplex apartment in Brooklyn and owned a house in Hyannis.

"No, I'm happy," I lied.

There was no point in currying favor or disfavor. Let her win the argument. There are no room/board charges if she wins the argument. If she loses and you win, then you lose because invariably you will pay.

"Yes, you're right, perhaps the rubber business is not very prestigious."

"Maybe you should try hosiery?"

"Sure."

"They give you pensions in the hosiery business. You don't get that with condoms. Besides, what's a nice Jewish girl working with rubbers?"

It's true. My friends were lobbyists for gun companies or copy editors for clients who made butter. It was a small world, and they all knew each other, and gave each other jobs, though not me.

"I have some friends in the hosiery business. Did you go to college?" she asked.

"Yes."

"Where?"

"Staten Island State."

"Is that why you're working with rubbers?"

"No, my father said it would help diminish my anger toward men."

"What does that mean?"

"He said that if I could appreciate that their lives depend on a small piece of synthetic material, I could understand their vulnerability."

"You're not a lesbian, are you?"

"No."

"Good, I don't like lesbians. I think my ex daughter-in-law is one." Lavina turned red like her Subaru.

Lavina was rather insistent, in general. She was particularly insistent that her neighbor, a "New age dyke who is a smart business woman," was responsible for the backward spiral of Lavina's once sanctimonious rule over a people-free neighborhood on their Hyannis street.

The woman had a Jack Russell who barked nonstop.

"Shut the fuck up!" Lavina yelled at the wooden house where the canine lived. The house had been built by a gluten-free construction company and you could hear everything outside.

She was annoyed at this "dumb *shiksah*" for a multitude of reasons, and most recently, because the woman was "opening another store in Hyannis."

It was unclear where Lavina's antipathy toward lesbians and their money originated.

Lavina's former daughter-in-law, whom she accused of being a "radical gay," said Lavina "molested" her kid.

"All I did was spank the girl. These politically correct types," she said, "are worse than Stalinists." Lavina had family members murdered by Stalin, which gave her a bitter view of anything that "veered near communist ideology."

As for "molesting her granddaughter," Lavina was more a disciple of brain molestation. She could take your brain and make you feel as if she were your resident lobotomist.

Her "brain molestation" techniques were also in her art—abstract blue and green smegma patterns—she captured the essence of smegma in batik.

A critic in *Art News* had written, "Lavina Schwartz is more on top of this subject matter than Philip Roth."

"That's what we have in common," I mentioned to Lavina, "I work with rubbers, and you concern yourself with what goes outside of them."

"You know *nothing* about my work!" she hissed. "You know zero about the theoretical precedence of smegma and its expression through batik."

"But I work with rubbers," I added, quietly.

"You're just a blue-collar factory worker."

There were a few moments of silence.

"I'm sorry," she glanced at me, "did I offend you?"

It's very characteristic of me not to defend myself. I lapse into passive/aggressive inarticulateness, which causes the said person who has caused me neurological pain to suffer.

"No," I replied, "I'm just in the middle of a Philip Roth book and I'd like to finish it."

"Oh—which one is that?"

"The Breast."

"Is that where the main character gets breast cancer?"

"No, it's about a man who turns into a breast."

"Oh… " Her "oohs" were self-effacing. You knew, and she knew, the argument, like a tedious chess game, had not gone in her favor.

"Have you gotten your bus schedule for tomorrow?" she asked me, "I won't be able to drive you."

"Yes."

"Good."

"Remember," I said to myself, as I took *The Breast* to bed, "nothing in this world is free, and when it is, it is insufferable."

PETER

rob roensch

1. Peter told the teacher he didn't mean to fall into the shark and ray tank at the aquarium field trip, that he just leaned over too far and lost his balance, but I was watching, and I know. We became friends.

2. Peter and I were both altar boys. Peter's mom made him wear shiny black shoes but my mom let me wear my cleanest sneakers.

3. Peter proved he could fit his entire body into a locker.

4. Peter listened to Creedence Clearwater Revival because his father did. He hated his father.

5. Peter only smoked pot during school.

6. Peter kissed his dog on the nose.

7. Peter offered to share the Reese's Pieces he'd pocketed at the 7-11 but I wouldn't take any. "You know you're going to hell anyway," he said, "if that's what you think makes the difference."

8. When I said I had homework, Peter opened his hands.

9. When I wanted to go home, Peter flew past the exit.

10. When I fell asleep, I awoke surrounded by houseplants.

A. "You read too much," he says.

B. "Jesus was basically born in a 7-11," he says. He looks deeply at his half-gone Cherry Dr. Pepper.

C. "You think important things only happen to other people and in other places," he says.

A story: it's past midnight on a cold clear night in early winter in Boston and we're wandering, his mom's station wagon is parked illegally by the river two miles away, I've got six dollars and I'm pretty sure Peter has nothing. He's bareheaded, talking fast. The windows of the bars we walk past glow with a yellow beery warmth; we'll never be inside again. Coming towards us on the sidewalk is a crooked, stumbling man in at least three sweatshirts and as we are we are even with him he looks up and in a yellow-mouthed, no-eyed moment something happens and he falls and flails into us, into me, and I'm already pushing him off but I don't have to because Peter has collected him in his arms. The man smells like rot, even in the cold. His feet are slipping in the smeared flurries, seeking the level, and Peter doesn't let go, holds him up. I see Peter press his face into the man's shoulder. When the man is standing on solid ground, Peter lets him go.

Ten years later I was nowhere near the ocean and had not heard Peter's voice for five years.

Twenty years later I find myself standing in Target appraising a sleek box containing an apparatus for hanging an expensive television on a wall. The thin young man who pointed me to the correct aisle, I see after he turns back to his register, has Peter's constellations of acne on his cheeks, Peter's goofily arctic blue eyes but not Peter's manner, Peter's wild complete attention. My five-year-old, gleeful weirdo, stands at my knee gnawing on the elephant we keep telling her not to gnaw on. There's rain in my hair still. I have so much and am so bereft.

I don't believe what they said happened in that Burger King, in that motel room. Whatever was, there must have been a moment when a word, a breath's work, would have mattered.

Loss is like a gift. Here, you, right now, open your arms to hold this specific empty space.

The only prayers I believe are lists:

O what silver the lines on the roads in the twilight and rain.

O what gentle green mucked water lapping at the edge of the awkward lake like the lake itself is taking little wet breaths.

O what the chill air is coming from the July parking-lot into the mall, your hands and face and fingertips filmed with sweat and dust.

O the infant asleep in the clear plastic box; O the daylight that is this moment lingering in a city a day's drive to the West.

O let me again peel open the tube of tennis balls and fire them one by perfect one thunking against the side of the second-best pizza place with my friend Peter.

A. Would anyone listen if I said a few words over the PA?

B. Why are there so many different kinds of lightbulbs?

C. What is a soul? What do for example I contain?

10.   I can be both soft-spoken and firm when I crouch near my writhing child complaining for a box of the cereal that looks like tiny waffles.

9.   I remember Peter.

8.   I do not wear sneakers to church.

7.   I do not always wear safety goggles when I operate power tools.

6.   I am vain about the whiteness of my teeth.

5.   I have a daughter and a son and a wife and a mother and a father.

4.   I read too much and am often ungenerous with my time.

3.   I can pull my thumb out of its socket and put it back in with minimal pain.

2.   When I was thirty-one and about to no longer take care of only myself, I was driving through an unfamiliar city at dusk and slowed to turn into a 7-11 for a bottle of water when a shirtless teenager on a BMX appeared flying out of an alley and before I could come to a stop he clipped my bumper and soared awfully into the street. When I tell the story people assume he was on something, because of the circumstances, but I can't say because I don't know. All I know is what I saw and what I did. I got out of the car. I was there kneeling beside him in the street as he gathered himself to half-sitting, moaning, and discovered the wrist he was already cradling in his lap like a baby was broken. "Hell were you?" he said, his eyes squeezed closed against the pain.

"He came out of nowhere," said a deep voice just across the street, a silhouette in the light of an open door of a car jerked to a halt. "These kids are lunatics."

I laid a hand on the bare knob of the young man's shoulder and he did not shake it free or even, to tell the truth, appear to notice. He shivered and breathed.

"It's okay," I said. "It's okay."

1.   I no longer refuse to acknowledge that I have intimations that every ordinary moment is a birth and a death and an emergency.

HOLY THOUGHTS

christina dalcher

Peek-A-Boo in the Pew

I've become something of an underwear connoisseur since I took this gig. My bet's on baby blue cotton this morning, which is okay, but not as good as red satin.

Even the best Catholic girls don't come to mass on a weekday, not unless there's a May Queen crowning or Wednesday night choir practice or their parents forced confession on them for one or another venial sin. Weekday masses are for ladies with blue hair and widows with moth-eaten wigs and people who think they're gonna die soon.

But Anne-Marie's here in the front pew every Tuesday, seven sharp, that pleated plaid skirt rolled up at her waist, three inches of pink skin between knee socks and hemline screaming *Hello, world!* before school starts. She's here because I'm the early-riser altar boy; I'm the early-riser altar boy because Anne Marie's mother hates crowds and switched Sunday for Tuesday. Also, Tuesday mass is a lot shorter.

We aren't actually dating, not in the strict sense of the word, not unless you count last summer's barbecue in the Wilsons' backyard when I walked up to Anne Marie with a hot dog and asked if she knew a good place to hide something about that size. Probably not my finest hour, since Anne Marie's dad was standing behind me. Since then, I don't get to see her much.

Which doesn't mean I don't get to see much of her on Tuesday mornings.

Right at that part when Father O'Sullivan starts his frankincense parade down the aisle, up the aisle, back down the aisle, right when the blue-haired ladies and the people with cancer prayers start coughing up a lung, that's when she does it. Those pink knees open up like Moses' Red Sea. And speaking of red—

Peek-a-boo-boo-*baby*. It ain't no reflection from the stained glass. This is real red satin today. Satan's panties to the max.

The thing about a cassock, the preferred costume of all altar boys, is the convenience factor. Lean a little forward to minimize the tent-pole effect those red undies bring on, feint a reach for the bell on your right side, slide your left hand under and up. Like they say, the right hand doesn't need to know what the left is up to.

Anne Marie stares piously into her bible and closes up the peephole the second Father O'Sullivan's done with his incense cloud business. That's all right. I got the mental picture down.

The only thing I don't like about Tuesday morning mass is that it's always over way too soon, even with the addition of that frankincense shit Father O'Sullivan started—at my suggestion, of course. Some of the congregation have to get to their doctor's appointments, Anne Marie's mother needs to get her hair done, and Anne Marie has to roll her skirt back to regulation length and high-tail it off to school.

Stuff that Might Fit in a Yarmulka

Ruthie Steinbaum's right boob. Ruthie Steinbaum's left boob. Ruthie Steinbaum's sister's right boob. The freckled girl who works at the library's left boob. Sharon Stone's right boob.

Well, you get the idea. Who cares if Sharon Stone isn't Jewish?

Today's lesson at my yeshiva is on piety, which is a fancy word for tradition, which in turn is a fancy word for do whatever the fuck the Rabbi says and don't ask questions. We're rubbing our kippahs and fingering our prayer shawls and twirling our earlocks while we read from the Talmud about the fear of heaven and while Rabbi Moshkovsky rambles on about how many cubits some old fart would walk without his head covered. But everyone in the room is thinking the same thing: that night we caught a glimpse of Ruthie Steinbaum undressing.

Since then, it's real hard to consider a skull-cap without thinking about boobs.

A Short List of Other Things I Could Do Five Times A Day

I'm not saying I don't want to pray anymore. Praying's cool, saves your soul, gets you eternity in the light. So I'll still pray, it's just that with all that time in between, there are a few activities I'd like to try:

1. Kiss each one of Naflah's toes.
2. Lead Naflah into the desert so I can watch her make sand angels in what passes for snow.
3. Monkey-scramble up a palm tree and shake shake shake until dates rain on Naflah like fat drops of sweetness.
4. Transform myself into a tube of henna, a bottle of her nail lacquer, her comb.
5. Not think about Naflah.

STAGES OF MAN
alice kaltman

Little White Lie

On the morning of his Bar Mitzvah David Leibowitz stood in front of his sister's full-length mirror. He turned sideways and swiveled from the waist up, like a starlet photographed on the red carpet. With pursed lips and head in a come-hither tilt, he imagined himself in a little black dress. His body was still a scrawny asexual thing so the imagining didn't require much morphing. Today David would become a man and he felt more like a woman than ever. He'd thought about becoming a Bar Mitzvah his entire life. The last year had been a real cluster fuck, what with all the preparation; the Hebrew classes, the Havtarah tutorials, all the talk at home and at synagogue of what it meant to be a man.

David's relief came in furtive fantasies. The one he returned to most often was of himself as herself, on the dance floor at the Bar Mitzvah reception, grinding up against Chucky Weintraub, a boy David had fostered a painful crush on since 3rd Grade. Fantasy David's hair was waist long and professionally straightened. She wore mascara and coral lipstick. Her nails were French manicured. She had on the standard Bar Mitzvah uniform; spaghetti-strapped ebony sheath, Tiffany bracelet, and ballet flats because every prepared girl knew you needed a pair to change into if you really wanted to dance. High heels were for the ceremony and photos, only.

What was David? He didn't know for sure, yet. Honestly, everyone turned him on. Girls, boys, women, men. Agnes, his 20-something piano teacher; lovely, willowy, smelling like lilacs. Rabbi Levinson, the youngest rabbi at Temple Emanuel with his beautiful smile and hairy forearms. Gwen Harris from Bio class, with her boobs and bossypants attitude. David loved looking at boobs but was that because he wanted a pair himself or because he wanted to squeeze someone else's? All David knew was he wasn't a man, had no inclinations to be manly. David felt like an un-man, if that was something.

David had his speech memorized, a bland treatise on *Derech Eretz* the moral law that says, "We must conduct ourselves in a way that does not offend those around us." In his speech David would spin *Derech Eretz* to be about acceptance; let people be whatever they want to be as long as they don't hurt anyone else. He was hoping to plant some seeds.

David pulled himself from his confusing reflection. He made sure the door was locked before he walked over to his sister's dresser and removed a pair of underwear from her lingerie drawer. He'd coveted this particular pair for months. Ivory satin bikinis, with a delicate little bow.

"*Emet*," David whispered to himself as he slipped on the panties. *Truth*. One must always tell the truth according to the Torah, although a little white lie is okay if it preserves the peace. For the time being, until truth was possible or even known, David would keep a little white lie comfortably hidden behind the zipper of brand new Bar Mitzvah slacks.

Everything and Nothing

"To each his own penis," Abe whispered to Isaac, who lay spread eagle and oblivious on the changing table. No mohel, no ceremony, no double edged knives. Abe was glad he and Sara finally laid the issue to rest. He could care less if his son had a penis like his own. He was fine with something less sculpted, less Yid, more Euro.

Isaac was only three days old, so tiny Abe could cradle his sacred skull in the palm of his hand while Isaac's body slumped like a hacky sack along Abe's forearm. His rose and cream cheese scented boy. His sweet, alien creature. This would be father and son's first diaper change without the hovering intervention of beloved wife and mother who, sleep deprived and sore nippled, had finally conked out in a face plant on the couch.

Abe pulled back the taped tabs on Isaac's disposable diaper as delicately as his cloddish, fat fingers allowed. How was it possible for such a featherweight angel to create, then expel so much liquid? Abe tossed the soggy loaded diaper in the bin and tried not to think about the pollution, the waste, the synthetics.

Abe gazed down at Isaac's uncut nobbin. Such a sweet bump of flesh atop bulbous scrotum. A little rosy dollop. For how many days had Abe's own penis looked like this, before his was trimmed according to Jewish law?

Isaac began to stir as soon as the air chilled his sodden junk. He wiggled tiny taloned fingers and noodled his hands towards his face. His peach lumpy body curled like a fern leaf, hugging inward, searching for itself. Isaac wailed and every muscle in Abe's body seized in response. The son's screeches created a maelstrom so deep in his father it was as if a sinkhole swallowed every bit of reason the man had left. It seemed impossible to think clearly, futile to attempt a simple task, like changing a diaper.

Isaac would wake Sara if he didn't stop crying. Abe had to act. He managed to wedge his hand between his son's writhing arms and legs, his hairy bear-like paw so ungainly and grotesque against Isaac's willowy limbs. Isaac's miraculous heart beat like moth wings, his papery eyelids so transparent and otherworldly. Abe's palm came to rest on the mound of Isaac's smooth warm gut, his tiny belly pillow. Everything and nothing held right there.

Abe massaged Isaac's tummy in gentle circles, easing what Abe had come to realize three days into fatherhood, was probably just a bit of irksome gas, a dinky air bubble trying to make its way up and out as a burp, or down and out as a fart.

Abe's fingers, large and indelicate, did the trick. A fart. Isaac calmed from the sense of skin on skin. Father to son. Son to father. The end to the beginning. The beginning of the end.

WE'D BE SOLDIERS

cade hagen

Our assignment was war. It was announced weeks earlier, and we'd thought of little else in the time between. The older ones did it all the time, but they shooed us away when we asked about it. Mr. Eriks told us to refer to him for the day only as Captain Eriks. Greg asked if we could call him Cappy, and Mr. Eriks said goddammit! He told us that he really was a captain in the wars that reset the world. He talked about the time before the wars often and with disdain, spitting and wincing like his mouth was filled with shards of bitter charcoal. Some of us would emulate the spitting, and he'd smile, bob his head in approval. Now the day had come, and we were split into two groups, thirteen on each side. Team 1 and Team A. I was A. He'd be our leader, and Mr. Harris (Captain Harris) would lead Team 1. Our respective captains corralled us onto opposite ends of the field, a hundred yards separating the factions. Our captain spoke.

"In war," he said. "In war." He nodded and spit, pacing in front of us, tracing the etches that paved his treebark face like lines of sap. We knelt before him. "In war, it's fuck them. You understand?"

"Fuck them," we chanted.

"Fuck them." Pacing and tracing and spitting. His voice pulsed thick and tarry like with cigar smoke, but he had no cigar. Pockets of saliva popped with his words. "The enemy? Those shitbirds on the other side of the field? They're animals. They're subhuman. They're dickless pieces of shit, understand?"

Greg snickered. We were nine.

"They're dogs," Captain Eriks said.

I liked dogs, but I knew what he meant. Still, those were my friends on the other side of the field.

"They hate you. They hate you." Spitting and pacing, spit black and smoky. "They hate you."

"Fuck them," we chanted. It was fun. Captain Eriks made it fun, made it real. It was a game, but it felt real. Fuck them. We'd kill them. We'd kill them with our cap guns. And then we'd have lunch with them in the cafeteria. But first, we'd kill them.

"Kill them," our captain said. "This is war. Do you understand? Do you understand?"

"Fuck them."

"Louder."

"Fuck them!"

"Louder!"

"FUCK THEM!"

They were my friends, and I wanted to kill them. I wondered if they wanted to kill me. From across the field, from Team 1 and Captain Harris, the wind gusted the hollow remnants of thirteen nine-year-old boys' unison fuck them. I guessed they did. But it was a game, and we'd have lunch after. They were my friends, but I felt a stirring, a burning, a satisfying collective ache radiating from Captain Eriks onto me. It swarmed and tickled, and I felt my faction feel it, too.

"Kill them."

A gunshot. I didn't know from where, but we heard it, and we knew what it meant. We charged. Cap rifles at the ready, we charged, prepared to fall fairly when our enemies' harmless orange nibs of gunpowder announced our death, prepared to force our enemies to fall fairly when our gunpowder announced theirs.

The first cap popped, a fraction of a real gun's crack. The second and third, ninth and tenth, pop pop pop. Fractions of real, fragments of real, whispers of the real wars that reset the world, that would reset it once more.

Benson, a friend I planned to eat lunch with, shot me. It was clear, plain as pudding, and despite the rules, despite what I thought I was prepared to do, I did not fall fairly. I could not.

I looked around. Nobody fell fairly.

"Fall, you fucker!" Benson said.

I heard my captain in my head. I would not fall.

"No!"

Benson shot again, and again I said, "No!" He shot until his caps were expelled, and I did the same. Ten feet between us, we shot until shooting was no longer an option. There was a moment, a flash, when decisions were made. It was war. We raised our wooden rifles from the barrels like maces, heavy stocks extended. I saw Benson's look. I felt my own. I felt that collective from my captain. Fuck them. We charged and swung. Benson missed; I didn't. The clack against the side of his skull satisfied, tremored up my arm, and I swung again, as satisfying as the first.

Benson went down, and I yowled a warrior's cry.

Captain Eriks wouldn't wince and spit charcoal when he spoke of me.

I heard the same clack of wood against bone chirping around me, somehow louder than the shouts and curses that went with it. I saw my friends fall, but not fairly. There was blood and there were tears and screams. I watched and as I watched the collective emptied from my gut and left behind a sickness, a nausea, a worm that wriggled with the wrongness. What had we done?

Captain Eriks saw it, too. He ran toward us and saw what he'd caused, how immediately out of control it had gotten, and I could only imagine his fear and regret. He'd tried to make it real for his students, and he'd succeeded too much. I hated him for it. My friends. I swore I saw the regret in his eyes as he ran toward us, metal whistle dangling from his cracked lips, screeching.

"Stop!"

Like a recording, we stopped.

He stood before us and assessed. Three unconscious. Five rolling and moaning in reddening blades of grass. The rest brandishing wooden toys unfit for the snarls and rage that propelled them. The sound of breathing and moaning, of too much success. What have I done, I imagined our captain thinking. But then I saw his eyes and saw I was wrong and I didn't want to be part of his collective and he said: "Fuck them. Well done."

IN MEMORIAM FORMICARUM

hun ohm

—for EP

We were unkind to the ants. They weren't usually to blame. Though on occasion one might crawl up a pant leg and compel a dance or lodge its mandibles into our flesh when we moved to crush them, these transgressions were excusable, merely sins of instinct, while our own base ambitions were wanton and without clear redemption.

They weren't much to look at, the ants, and that's perhaps what made sport easy. That fifth-grade summer, we honed our creativity through trial and error, a seemingly endless supply of six-legged offerings. We chased them with stones and matchsticks and our own eager fingers. We learned to lightly maim them to make collection easier. Over and over we forced them to wander through the desolate wilderness of a sandbox. We blew sandstorms and summoned tsunamis with a garden hose. We raised our palms aloft, and sand poured from the sky in biblical proportions. In the quiet aftermath we held our breath until the ants reemerged to our shame and delight, digging frantically through the grainy ruins of their world before scrambling in vain for cover.

For those who dared withstand these tribulations, we celebrated their resilience with further sacrifice, tossing them onto the spider's lair where their shivering summoned the funnel weaver from its cone, and we would howl with glee when the spider pounced.

"Lord have mercy," the deacon's son Simon Keats was wont to say, and he would cross himself with one hand while his other plump fingers reached to knead more ants into submission. Simon was two years older and near the worst among us, savoring the finer points of a medieval ingenuity he spent many a Sunday perfecting. It was Simon who understood the viscosity of red

Jolly Rancher spit that he used to mire his hapless victims. It was Simon who looked to the skies for inspiration. Under Simon's tutelage, we learned how to harness the sun with a magnifying glass. He taught us to luxuriate in the zigzag pursuit of our quarry, to embrace that exquisite circle of sunshine that could crackle at any moment as it stalked and narrowed into incandescence, and the acrid fumes rose into the heavens above.

"That don't smell right," the acolyte Mikey Carlson said, his eyes still filled with silvery stars from the hunt's glow.

"You get used to it," Simon said. He breathed in deeply. "That's so. Go on, give it another shot." And Mikey Carlson did, as did all of us in our turn, our lips sealed tight with concentration. We set another offering in place, and then another, each ant shriveling more quickly than the one before as we eventually caught the hang of the perfect angle.

After a long afternoon in the wasteland, once the spider had its fill and the sun fell too low to provide sufficient warmth, Simon sculpted a mound of sand, sturdy and tall. He flattened the peak and wedged a pair of gray skipping stones atop it. Then Simon uncapped a can of no-drip spray paint usually reserved for model rockets and shook it vigorously to make the pea chatter. We watched solemnly, saying nothing, and Simon placed one of the last survivors on the slabs. Even though the perpetual motion of its limbs had long lost steam, we knew the will to beat the final rap remained intact for even this, the littlest of earthly things. An antenna twitched, sensed that the coast seemed clear, and the ant began to traverse down the slope. The motion caught Simon's all-seeing eye, and he rattled the can with one last flourish before pressing the nozzle down. Clouds of gold hissed out.

"Nowhere to run, no place to hide!" Simon cried when the ant scrambled left and right while the gold rained down upon it. Simon was generous with his application, and soon even the mound was shimmering like Yukon dust. Sweet, burning fumes wafted through the air.

"Goodness, that's pretty," Simon said after he released the nozzle, and the world grew silent, all of us awaiting the bounties of his good work. The ant scurried off the mount in one last mad dash for salvation that was almost there. Then the quick dry kicked in, and its desperate strides grew less pronounced, slowed, then finally froze.

"Now you know," Simon proclaimed. He lifted the ant with his fingertips and blew the last specks dry. And we saw that the ant was small. It was gold. Simon's fat pinky was delicately extended.

"That don't look right," Mikey said, though he reached out his palm to receive it.

"It's in the eye of the beholder," Simon reminded Mikey. He placed the first ant into Mikey's cupped palm and readied the slabs for an encore. "Go on," Simon said to Mikey, passing the can to him. "Show us. Let's see."

DWINDLE, PEAK, AND PINE

timston johnston

—with thanks to the Columbus Zoo

We find Hay-Zeus on what we think is a Sunday. He is in Cruciform. He is missing below the chest, his neck gnawed away. His fists clench fur. Shame, another says. He is our cook and we have not eaten since what we think was Friday. Not fish nor frog nor worm. Here, knowing what will come, we cannot harbor a small roasting fire. But we do. We cover Hay-Zeus' eyes with mud and grass, lay a flank along his lips. We pick at him, grateful he has given us another last meal.

You can die, they say, strapped down, or you can die *tango en masse au-nature*. We had read of the hanged, the electrified, the burned and shot, those lacerated, those blindfolded at stakes. We have studied the injection, and we say we've never been fond of sleep; even there, we knew what waited upon waking. So we choose exile. So we choose the tiger. Because there is hope, we say to the cameras. There is chance. There is freedom. And because, we say, some of us rather the pain.

Our choice is to bind but not to bond. Together, we've built huts on higher ground, on the steeper of the foothills. We've taken to sleeping in the trees. If we walk north, one faces south. We hunt as we are hunted, and when the tiger feasts at night, a boat will arrive in the morning. Upon it, another life foregone, another name to forget.

We have lost our arsonist, so we have lost our fire. In the past, he had killed sixty-three, and ever since he went foraging alone, he has doomed fourteen more.

The tiger knows the innocent, says Alma, while our jury of peers does not. Judgment, we say, does not come from those like us. You are the cotton, we say, sopping up the guilt the jungle has washed from the rest of us. The blood once under our nails is now yours. The tiger smells this and has for miles now. So stand there, we say, and return to tell us how hunger is stymied by the righteous.

When Grigori takes ill, we tell him letting had always worked, it's only that everything else worked better. Now, we say, we have no everything else; what we have is leeches. One to the ankle for returned balance, one to the temple to draw this sickness through the mind, and one to the sternum so that they may know their god. Let the others go where they will, we say, as we have. You will grow weak, we say, but your strength will return with sleep. In that time, we will not abandon you. When you wake from the fever, you will see us here. You will know us as the trees.

In one more stand-off, Lélek breaks the tension by collapsing and vomiting mud and water. We pull him up, say, we do not bow to death; we face it. Stand here with the wronged on your breath, with their voices whispering your sins; stand here with what pride remains and wait for her decision. Open your palms and join us in saying, *Well?*

THE MOON

bud smith

We met at a planetarium. I was on parole and getting blood tests every month. I'd started doing LSD as often as possible because it didn't show up on their tests, and I still needed to live on a different world.

The sidewalk splitting apart, I walked two miles in the rain to attend the laser light show. When I got there, I found out I was mistaken, like I often am. I paid the six dollars to the ticket taker and went in and looked at fake versions of the real stars projected on a big domed black nothing.

There was only one other person in the amphitheater. I was tripping so hard, I sat down right next to her and leaned over and said, "Where's the lasers?" She said, "You're soaking wet." I took off my shirt and she howled with joy.

After the show we went out to her white Mustang and screwed on the hood of the car. Nobody cared about us. Then we sat in the car for hours, just talking, mostly talking about how nobody on Earth cared about us, a popular topic. The engine was off. The windows fogging up. I could see and feel the world disappearing. Jane said she had simply replaced a vodka problem with fucking, the same way that some people replace *the whatever ails ya* with Jesus. Or with tennis. Or with suicide. She said it was a shame she had met me now, she felt a real connection to me, and would like to be exclusive, and in love or something like it. She said it was sad.

"Sad why?"

"Oh, sad because I'm leaving."

I had a job at a medieval-themed gas station. Nobody else would hire me. I had to wear a plastic suit of armor. Two days after our initial meeting at the planetarium, Jane pulled up to the pump and I filled her tank, but I had my visor down, she didn't know it was me. She was so kind to this stranger in the suit of plastic armor. I'd never met a kinder more gentler person. I decided then that I would do anything with her, that I would go anywhere with her, long as I had a chance. I called from the payphone on my break, I told her that. We were together that night, and most nights after that for a while.

Before our date that night I had group therapy in the basement of the Lutheran church. The sleepy-eyed counselor had a watermelon. When the watermelon was passed to you you were supposed to speak about your feelings. He said the watermelon was like a big egg and inside the big egg was either a monster or an angel. You'd get into big trouble if you smashed the watermelon, so nobody did that. We talked when we had the watermelon and we were obligated to go into greater detail than we had when we'd held the grapefruit, when we'd held the apple before that, when we'd held a single grape and just said our name. Here's what I learned, overall—everyone just wants what they want but it's all ambiguous, even to them, no one really knows what they want, they just long for it, and it is invisible and takes no form.

Jane met me at the shooting range. I thought I saw my parole officer at the soda machine but it turned out to just be a cardboard cutout of Charlton Heston. We peeled off all our bullets and then we had sex again on the hood of her car. Still, nobody cared about us. Afterwards, engine off, windows fogged up, she asked me what my Narcotics Anonymous meetings were like. I told her, "If I tell you I'll have to lobotomize you. She said that'd be alright. She wanted to stop feeling guilty anyway. She told me her AA meetings were very helpful up to the point they became biblical, but the thing that made it hard to not get drunk was that everywhere you looked there was some subconscious advertisement for liquor. Busses passing by in the shape of wine bottles. She said, "Earth is not the kind of place to get sober." I held her hand and told her that my meetings took place in an abandoned funhouse and that one of the guys was a speed freak who thought he was a werewolf, so whenever we were anywhere close to a full moon he didn't come in. It was for our safety. He didn't want to full moon kill us all. The counselor said, *Everybody here is a werewolf, okay? Everyone is cursed, is infected, has supernatural powers, knows what it is like to live between worlds.*

They took my blood. I pissed in a test cup. The nurse snipped a lock of my hair with a pair of rusty scissors. My eyes were dilated and she said, "I shouldn't even be letting you take this test, your eyes are as big as the Big Bad Wolf's."

I said, "If you want me to pop one of my eyeballs out for you to test, I'll do that."

She said, "That's not necessary. There's no eyeball analysis."

I got into trouble because I collapsed, foaming at the mouth, gun in pocket, in a playground with a rubber castle, was found there. My counseling had started out with the grape, like I said, then it was cherries. When you had the cherry in your hand you could speak about your substance(s). When we got a little better and were able to talk about bigger things, the cherry became an apple, and the apple was our regrets, our sins, so to speak. And then a grapefruit. By the time winter was over you could speak when the cantaloupe was in your hands, and you could blab on forever when you had the grapefruit, you were almost proud. I got real into things. I grew my beard out and started braiding it. Started microdosing with psilocybin. The gas station job encouraged we look the part. I've done a lot of things I'm not proud of. I've been better. I've been worse. I've thrown a couple pineapples at the wall.

Two junkies robbed the gas station. One had a knife. The other had a sawed-off shotgun. Which was funny, because all us worker bees had plastic swords. Plastic shields. Plastic war hammers. They made off with twelve hundred dollars. Two junkies, who died later that week. I used to know them both. Very well. A past life. An original design of the gas station included a metal dragon perched on top of the snack shop that would belch fire up into the sky so cars streaming by on the highway would see the spectacle and be compelled to take the offramp and investigate. In my experience, no one really knows what they are doing. Even the fire marshal.

Jane wanted to go camping, just the two of us, up in the mountains. I skipped my watermelon meeting in the basement of the Lutheran church. I drove to her house in my pickup. Her Mustang wasn't in the driveway.

She came out her door with a sleeping bag under her arm. She kissed my lips deeply, my head hanging out the window.

"Where's your Mustang?"

"Sold it."

"You sold it? I don't believe it."

"I ride my bicycle to work now. It's for the best, more exercise, you'll like the results, haha."

We went narrowly across state lines and I got a boner. I was breaking parole! The mountains. Ascension into the sky! We climbed out of the car. Jane got naked in the moonlight. My eyes were wide, studying the pale skin reflecting the moon back at itself and making her appear otherworldly.

"Forget that car, the bicycle is a good thing."

"I thought you'd say that."

We laid down on our sides in the soft grass and felt around for the switches on each other's bodies that would reveal all of the mysteries of light and horror, patience, doubt, desire and truth.

After we worked up a good sweat, we walked hand in hand down to the lake below and washed the sweat off. We swam out into the dark water with the stars and the moon shining down onto us, making everything shimmer.

That night, we slept in the bed of the truck, flat on our backs. Jane kept staring up at the sky, as if she was seeing it for the first time. She'd blink slowly, her eyelashes trailing behind her lids.

"I've always felt close to the moon."

"Yeah?"

"When I was a little girl, I had a dream every night about walking around on the moon. Living there. Having a life. Look at all of that light. Imagine being in the middle of that glowing?"

"It'd be nice, I suppose."

"To live in a dream."

"I want to leave, too," I said.

"You should," she said. "Where do you want to go?"

"I want to go down to South America and find the Ibioga tree."

"What's up with the Ibioga tree?"

"Gets you fucked up."

"Ah—maybe you'd be better off on a world where you couldn't get fucked up."

"I'd rather die."

My parole officer said, "Get the fuck out of here, I don't want to see you like this again. This is an insult!"

There was a for sale sign on her front lawn beneath the dying elm tree.

My heart fell sharply and broke another one of my ribs. My heart is a wrecking ball. Don't you have one like me? Doesn't yours swing wildly when given cause and create all kinds of internal damage?

"You're really going away," I said. She nodded. I said, "Still?"

"How many times and in how many ways do I have to tell you?"

I wanted to see Jane that weekend but she said she was busy. When I pushed the request, she got quiet and evasive.

"I have plans."

"Alright."

The way Jane handled it, how she anxiously changed the subject, fidgety and awkward, I figured I was probably 'the other guy'. Jane was important to me. Already my heart was like a stone falling and chipping the inside of my ribcage. She had a secret. I could tell that she was balancing me against the secret, seeing which would stick and which she would have to give up.

So, headlights off, I tailed her. She cruised ahead on her bicycle. Oblivious. Head in the clouds. I put my truck in neutral and coasted downhill through the sleeping town.

It surprised me when Jane took a turn down a quiet road, just past the abandoned Wicker World plaza, that I knew from experience led nowhere. She glided into a farther abandoned strip mall with a bowling alley and a Food Universe that'd been closed for some time.

But there were other other cars in the potholed lot.

I watched Jane lean her bicycle against the wall of the bowling alley. A beacon of light washed over her as she entered the door. The light snuffed out as the door closed on its own.

I parked and crept in behind her.

There was a group of people sitting in the bowling alley, having some strange meeting. A bald man with small spectacles, that made me think of a mole, stood in front of the crowd. He wore a button-up white dress shirt and had a lot of pens in his breast pocket. The pens made me think he was important for some reason. Through the crack of the door, I tried to listen but they were speaking too low. I watched the backs of their heads for a while, specifically, the back of Jane's head. Periodically I'd note that she would enthusiastically nod her head. What was she nodding about? A few minutes later, I saw her rise and ask a question. It nearly drove me insane not knowing what the question was. I should have crept closer, perhaps crawling on my belly like a boy playing soldier, infiltrating the enemy line—instead, I got nervous and left.

She was at my window late that night, pebbles bouncing off the glass. "You awake?"

"I am."

"Let me in."

I opened the window and she climbed into my room. Her body was warm and her neck was salty. "Do you still go to your AA meetings?"

"No. I told you. Too biblical."

"Okay, I thought you said that." The room was moving. Shadows eating other shadows. She pulled my underwear down and started jerking me off.

"I don't go to church, this feels better." She climbed on top of me and for the first time in months I wished I was sober so I could feel what it felt like to be normal. To be an earthling.

That weekend, again, she was too busy to see me. I couldn't figure her out. Hot. Then cold. I stumbled into her neighbor's yard and puked everywhere. Then I saw she was having a yard sale. She was selling everything she owned. I hid behind the trash cans and watched for what could have been ten minutes or ten hours. Soon she was alone and surrounded by dishes and cups and jackets and vinyl records and Ikea furniture. I crossed the street.

"I followed you, once."

"What?"

"To the old bowling alley on Mill Road," I said.

"Oh."

She admitted, "I was worried about this conversation."

"What were you doing there?"

"If I told you, you'd think I was nuts."

"Try me."

"Okay. Come in the house."

We left all the things out there on the lawn, unattended. She shut the front door and looked out the bay window. No one was coming anyway.

"Just say it quick, like pulling a band aid off. Zip. It won't hurt as much."

She turned to look at me. "I'm in a destructive moon cult, I told you this."

"Heh?"

But then she couldn't look at me. "It's like talking to a wall. You're tripping out again? What's it this time? Mushrooms? Salvia? Banana peels?"

"Six purple gel tabs, no big deal."

"I belong to a sect and we worship the moon, I don't know how to put it any other way."

"A moon cult?"

"Ha! A moon cult! No, I don't think I'd call it a moon cult, it's not that at all… well, uhhhh, maybe it is kinda a moon cult."

"Alright."

She'd sold her Mustang, gave them the money. Her house was just about to close with a realtor. She was giving the money to them too.

"For what?"

"We're going to the moon."

"You're gonna fly a spaceship to the moon?"

"Not exactly. Come with me."

"I couldn't."

"I want you too."

She was brainwashed. There was no way of talking any sense into her about it. I knew what I had to do. It was simple, I just had to go with her to her next meeting and grab that mole-faced man with all the pens and get him to—to what?

I'd just shake the living hell out of him. If that didn't work, I'd start punching. That always seems to help.

I drove Jane up into those same mountains. There was a large structure there now. A bridge that went up above the pine trees a hundred feet, stopping at the mouth of the night sky.

"Thanks for the ride," she said. "I wish that you'd change your mind and come with us. I really love you."

The people were all standing around in a cluster, looking up at the sky. As we got nearer, I noticed the serious man with all the pens consulting a chart of stars. He'd look at the map and then look at the tree-line, back to the map and then up at the full moon.

"Yup, tonight's our night."

There was excitement in the air, as if those were people waiting on the dock for a cruise ship that would take them on a voyage around the tropics. They smiled, standing tall with their suitcases, all silently wondering, "Do I have all I'll need for the moon?"

I was about to go over and start shaking the mole man until all his pens fell out of his pocket.

But, as predicted, the moon appeared to be getting bigger and bigger. Swelling up. Getting closer and closer. The people went like this, "Oooooow!"

"Ahhhhhhn!"

"It's coming!"

A few of the more eager ones began to clap and jump up and down. Jane grabbed onto me so hard that her fingernails went into my forearm and nearly raised blood. I didn't notice. I was staring up at the sky. The moon swelled and swelled and a light came over us, so white and blinding that it was hard to keep my eyes open. I had to peek through the bottom of my eyelids.

Like an orange hanging from a tree, the moon was then immediately over us. Some of the people went up the structure and simply stepped onto the moon.

"I'm going," she said. "But you should come."

"Where?"

"Up into the sky and then space. Who knows after that?"

"I'm not sure."

She took my hand and we went up the structure. She led me like a child walking with a balloon. Then, she let go of my hand and stepped onto the moon.

"Don't be scared," she pleaded. I let go of her hand. She stepped onto the moon and I stood there on the platform, having made my decision.

"Jump!"

I shook my head and the moon started going up and up and up. She got smaller and it got smaller. Until it was up in the sky, just a speck. I was off parole. I didn't have to pump gas anymore in a suit of plastic armor. Watermelons were just watermelons again.

FUR

samuel j. adams

I jilted a lover once—I was caustic, young, and cold and I didn't think things through—and a few days after the jilting this lover left a dead squirrel on my doormat, a chubby and fluffy Eastern gray slashed open at many angles to dispel the calm of a silver-lighted Sunday morning in mid-October. The doorbell rang and I stepped outside and bloodied my sheepskin slippers in dead squirrel parts. I saw her Volvo speed off, filling the street with the goosey honking of its horn. I wrapped the squirrel carcass in the ruined doormat and tossed both in the trash. I didn't know what else to do.

I figured she left the first squirrel to shock and wound me. I mainly figured this because it worked. Squirrely got a raw deal, but I deserved something: the shock of a cute dead thing, the ruination of my favorite slippers. I had been a jerk and now I was chastened, and I resolved to be less of one.

I was surprised when the second squirrel came exactly one year later, this time without the fanfare of ringing doorbells and honking cars. The following year, she sacrificed a third squirrel to the same dark Gods of memory and resentment and delivered me the offering. After that, I bought a plastic doormat I could clean with a hose. Dead squirrels four and five arrived annually according to her bitter pattern.

But the sixth dead squirrel was different. It didn't look different—see one fuzzy bloody pile of tail and intestine and you've seen them all—but the context made it so. See, the squirrel-deliverer and I had been getting along. She'd taken a job working in the building across from mine and we were occasionally eating lunch together. She told me she was dating a nice guy named Craig, had a new dog, a promotion, and a submerged talent for watercolors she was happily rediscovering. Things seemed to be going well. I never brought up all the squirrels because I didn't think I'd have to. And yet when October 15th rolled around she commemorated it with another

{142}

sciurine slaughter. I'd watched for her at the window all morning, but when she arrived she looked so chipper and at ease setting down the mangled rodent I knew I couldn't confront her, break whatever spell guided her here. And anyway, the squirrel was dead.

Next time she saw me she greeted me warmly and we carried on like old chums. We ate sandwiches in the park where live squirrels darted about, moving happily unaware of the dangerous predator with the blonde highlights and a pink cardigan sitting in their midst. "Cute, aren't they?" she said. "Big old chubby-wubbys." My silence on the matters of these chubby-wubbys was rewarded with the continued pleasure of her company, and a seventh massacred mammal.

And in the 364 days between the dispersal of dead squirrels, we grew closer still. After the ninth dead squirrel, we tried dating again. After the tenth, I proposed. We wed two weeks before number eleven arrived.

Everybody says a successful marriage is about compromise, and here's ours: every year my wife leaves a dead squirrel on the doorstep to show me she is fine, and every year I pretend I believe her. Those are the conditions of unconditionality, of loving someone no matter what, even when "no matter what" has a body count of eleven dead squirrels.

But acceptance is one thing, hope entirely another, and I got a very simple hope: that some Sunday in mid-October, it'll be my wife standing pert and kindly outside the door instead of a lumpy and eviscerated squirrel. I'll open up the door and we will hold each other and she'll look at me with her shimmery jade-hazel eyes full of forgiveness or forgetting—I won't care which by then—and say, "Oh my love, my darling, I have no idea what those poor little squirrels ever could have done to make me so upset!"

But until that happens, every October there'll come a morning that finds me rinsing fur off my doormat, scooping up the pieces and feeling grateful for everything I've got.

THE MUSTACHE GAME

benjamin devos

My roommate Frank is playing the mustache game. The mustache game is when you stick a piece of tape to the television set, and every time the tape looks like a mustache on a person's face, you have to chug your beer.

It's just Frank playing alone, laughing and drinking.

He smells like beef vegetable soup and wears tighty-whities around the apartment.

He gets drunk every night, and then somehow wakes up earlier than me each day and sings loudly to himself while he has his morning poop.

Like he'll sing, "Poopin' in the mornin', consider this your warnin'."

Or, "Sometimes I pee when I poop but when I poop I pee, a brown log falls from between my cheeks to part the yellow sea."

Then a flushing sound.

I would rather die in my sleep than have to wake to one more of Frank's songs.

Living with Frank makes me realize that death is not the end, it is only the beginning.

I am almost certain that he is the reincarnation of some obnoxious creature, like a cockroach or a pigeon, which has been reborn into a higher lifeform but refuses to accept the responsibilities that come with it.

I sit at the table behind Frank, noticing my likeness as a shadow across his bald head.

I cast darkness everywhere I go.

Just nothing but gloom and disappointment.

Like a balloon of spoiled soup ready to pop.

"Frank, your scalp is especially shiny today," I say.

Frank says, "Yo, what are some words that rhyme with anal beads?"

He twists his head around, leaning back over the couch, clicking the aluminum beer can between his thumb and pointer finger.

"Um, how about shameful deeds," I say.

He says, "That's good, but I need something more visual. Laser beams, that's a good rhyme."

"Nice one," I say.

"Yeah man, I'm like writing a song and trying to figure out the chorus."

Frank has recently started going to open mics and playing songs he writes

All of his songs consist of a series of disjointed images.

When he sings, it's sort of a mumbling ramble.

His demeanor and delivery are a cross between that of a punch-drunk boxer and a backwater televangelist.

He says, "Anal beads the size of baseballs, laser beams in the dance hall."

Then he starts playing air guitar.

He runs his fingers down the invisible guitar neck and moves them around in a tickling motion that is supposed to represent a guitar solo that he is not capable of playing in real life.

"Nice one," I say.

A commercial comes on the television.

It shows a man and a woman.

They are both hungry and want to buy food.

The woman says, "You're not already fat enough?"

The man says, "Leave me alone, bitch."

The woman says, "Did I touch a nerve, fatty?"

"You have mental problems. You don't even know how to make a salad."

"I know how to make a salad."

"How do you make a salad?"

Their argument continues long beyond the length of a commercial.

The woman thinks that salads are made with lettuce, tomato, and sometimes cucumber.

The man thinks that salads are made with lettuce, tomato, and sometimes cucumber, but that it doesn't end there, and that there are unlimited additions that you can put on top of a salad.

The man gives up and says nervously, "As long as I can use my favorite brand of ranch dressing, then I am satisfied."

They settle their dispute and eat salad together on a table that is filled with hundreds of romantic, burning candles and has a ranch bottle as the centerpiece.

Frank cracks open another beer.

He mutes the television and uses the silence to give his own version of the characters' dialogue.

For the man on the screen, he says, "You lookin' good tonight, baby."

For the woman, he says, "Thanks, handsome. It's because I ain't wearing a bra."

The conversation gets increasingly sexual, even though both characters appear to be elderly, and in a hospital room waiting for serious results from the doctor.

He ends the scene with a fart joke.

Frank is so used to laughing at his own jokes that it isn't even sad anymore.

Franks says that some guy at the bar the other night told him that his jokes remind the guy of his dad.

I say, "Nice, that's cool Frank."

He says, "I always wanted to be a father, and it made me feel like maybe I could use my comedy to be like a father figure to other people."

"That's cool," I say.

"Crystal cool," he says.

Frank says, "If I ever become famous I think I would run for mayor, and just like, try to be a father for everybody living in the city, because there aren't enough fathers to go around, and many of the fathers that are around are shitty at it anyway."

"Wow," I say.

"Like seriously, and I would go around to different neighborhoods handing out presents to the good kids and spankings to the bad."

He chugs his beer, neck swelling like a pelican, his bald head in a million wrinkles.

"So if you were famous, you would basically become a semi-abusive version of Santa Claus with some political power, who focuses all of his time on fathering people who may or may not already have fathers of their own."

"Bingo," says Frank.

I take a beer out of the refrigerator and think about the day I signed the lease with Frank, and how many beers I must have had that day to make such a bad decision.

I think about all of the bad decisions I have made accumulating in a dark cloud of sadness that rains salty tears over my head, frozen tears the size of hail, pelting me until I collapse in a bloody puddle on the floor.

Frank laughs as the woman's face on the television aligns with the tape.

He finishes his beer.

"Beer goes down smoother the more you drink it," he says in a hoarse, too-many-cigarettes voice, "but I should probably stop because I have a job interview at the garbage factory tomorrow morning."

"What's a garbage factory," I say.

He stares at me blankly.

"It's like, you know," he motions at the ceiling, "where the garbage goes."

"Do you mean like a dump or some sort of recycling center?"

"It's like the place where you sort through the stuff that people throw away and make sure it's good enough to be resold. You can like shop there and buy used stuff there, I think, maybe."

"Wow," I say, "Nice."

"Yeah, it's cool," he says.

I imagine Frank sifting through beer cans and trash-juiced cardboard for empty whipped cream canisters so that he could inhale fumes through the nozzle.

For the minutes to follow, his garbage sorting abilities would be greatly enhanced.

Frank shares his philosophy about trash and life, and by the end, I feel like I am falling down an endless pit, at the end of which is a giant dumpster with teeth and fire coming out of the mouth.

He says, "I would never live in the suburbs. Nope. Not me. I don't want deer and rabbits digging through my garbage. I'd rather have a crackhead dig through my trash than a deer. A crackhead I can handle. You give a crackhead five bucks, he'll leave your trash alone. You go up against a deer, and you don't know what the fuck might happen."

"But you live in an apartment," I say, "You don't have to worry about any of those things because someone comes and takes the trash out for us."

Frank says, "I know, eh, it's ironic."

Then he sings, "I'm a lone star shining bright, a trash-eating possum in the night, singing until my last breath, drinking myself to death."

His song is sudden, sad, and surprisingly coherent.

"Is that what you think about yourself?" I say.

"No, that's my impression of a sad folk singer," he says. "Fuckin' hate folk music. It's like so not rock 'n' roll."

He laughs.

It seems like he is forcing his laughter.

He is hurting on the inside, I think, or he realizes that the lyrics are true.

Hang in there, Frank.

"She has a mustache," he says, pointing to the woman on the screen.

"Drink up," I say.

"Cheers," he says, taking a long drink, and beating his chest with his fist.

I say, "Frank, you really know how to live."

And just then, a child wearing a raincoat on the television screen lines up with the tape.

"Cheers," Frank says again, taking his last sip before crushing the beer can against his forehead.

Watching the television we say, "Cheers," back and forth to one another, staying on the same plane of one-worded conversation that feels safe, and warm.

I say it, then he does, then we drink beer.

This is the mustache game.

RECENTLY ADDED IN SHIT YOU WATCHED ON MOM'S CABLE WHEN YOU WERE DEPRESSED WHILE 'BETWEEN JOBS' LIVING AT HOME IN YOUR EARLY-TO-MID TWENTIES

brian alan ellis

Being a thirty-five year-old teenager may or may not be going okay, and all I have to show for it are dead dreams and season one of *Full House* on DVD, but living alone is rad because you're able to spread depression throughout an entire enclosure without bumming anyone else out, which is super liberating, though I do have a cat, and sometimes I'll randomly yell or make weird grunting noises just to remind myself that "Hey, I'm still alive," which the cat loves, and my current crush is the Internet tech support woman who made me feel like I mattered for 10-15 minutes, so I now pronounce us husband and Wi-Fi, though telling me I "won't be disappointed" is pretty much like calling my initial reaction towards everything a lie, which I find very insulting, so just accept me for who I am, which is a person so far removed from reality that they're being smothered by their own crippling despair, and let's be honest, you're kind of a villainous piece of shit if you smoke cigars, and you're kind of a villainous piece of shit if you use the word "erudite" in a sentence, especially when it's used in this sentence, and 2001 is my shit right now, and The Wayans Brothers are my shit right now, and using a phone that doesn't flip open is basic as fuck, and Funeral Fatties would be a good name for a hook-up site that featured only plus-sized goths, which I'm all about because death is chasing me, and so is the gap between how many people I follow on Twitter to the amount of followers I actually have, so maybe the Twitter Help Center can assist in my debilitating self-loathing, and oh shit I just scrolled past a list entitled "20 Forgotten 80s Stars" that showed a picture of Ralph Macchio and I very urgently whispered to myself, "I'll *never* forget the Karate Kid, motherfucker," and you know, it's kind of a bummer to have never won a martial arts tournament, but *Ocean's Eleven* is my shit right now, and AOL chat rooms are my shit right now, and you *can* go home again but it'll most likely be completely fucked, so "home" is basically wherever there are people trying crazy hard to get you to finally leave, because honestly, homeless people and feral animals are the true outsider artists, the real movers and shakers, though non-artists are generally the best kinds of species, and maybe my biggest attribute when it comes to friendship is that I make for a nice, empty garbage can people can scream into, and I'd give you a textbook example but I never bothered reading textbooks so you'll just have to trust me on this, yet somehow I'm missing the chromosome where being poor and having to work shitty jobs is some passing phase that's supposed to end in your twenties, so maybe one day I'll open a My Little Pony-themed pizza parlor called Broneys Calzoneys, or maybe not, because one of the hardest things about starting a business is probably the anxiety of having to remember the names of people you've hired while trying to suppress a nagging, destructive urge to just run away and go die somewhere alone, so yeah, I'd give it the old college try, which means I'll get drunk and overwhelmed and quit really early on, and 9/11 conspiracy theories are my shit right now, and the first Strokes CD is my shit right now, and I found it oddly funny that while yelling at my cat to stop showing her ass I was reaching into a bag to retrieve a handful of peanut M&Ms, and sure, not many things in life make sense, but unloading obscenities in a parking lot so does, and if you don't have a cupboard that when opened Little Debbie snacks just fall out and smack against your face then see ya later!

IN THE EVENT OF MY DEATH
(NANCY, DON'T READ)

mack eisenmann

Dear Funeral Director,

In the event I die on a bull running trip (possibly July 6th-14th), you could open the funeral by saying something like "we always said Travis was full of bull." This way, you could lighten the mood while making an edgy reference to how I died. The bull thing isn't very likely to happen, though, because Nancy hasn't found out about the trip yet and she'll probably shut it down. (Please don't let her see this letter.)

I have some ideas for other scenarios, too:

In the event I die on account of my peanut allergy, you could say "Travis sure was a *swell* guy" (Because peanuts make my throat swell up).

If lightning strikes me, say you are feeling "struck by emotion."

In the event I die anywhere near a whiteboard or chalkboard, say "Travis was a re-markable fellow." (I got that one off the internet. Would you need to cite that? Don't use it of so.)

If I get eaten by an animal or choke to death on food other than peanuts, you could open with "thank you very *munch* for being here." I'm not set on that one, though, so say it only if you like it.

I'll have a will made up one of these days, but in case I don't get around to it:

Nancy gets the house and the car and everything else. I'm thinking about buying a Porsche Boxster/Cayman, and if I do that will go to Wes. Everything else goes to Nancy, though, or if I'm not with Nancy it goes to whoever I'm with. (If you're reading this, Nancy, I'm sorry for writing that. You know I'd never leave you.)

If my boss Mr. Johnson is at the funeral, make sure to say something about my successful app/robot/security camera business. (I am planning to quit this

Friday, June 7th, so don't say anything about it if I die before then. It would be best to bring it up if I die a few months *after* this Friday, so I can really get my company going. Only say this if I die after August 7th or so, to be safe. By that point we'll know what business I decided to start, anyway.)

In the event that I die before Hassle and Hoff—I have one request about those funeral pamphlets they pass out to everybody with the dead person's picture and a bible verse on them. I'd like them to say "At last he gets some peace and quiet from those damned birds." (If you think somebody might not know my birds, can you put a picture of them in the pamphlets, too? And make sure to put their names in there so people can see them.) You don't need to put a bible verse on there.

You can put a bible verse in the pamphlet in the event that Nancy murders me. (Don't put too much weight on this if it doesn't happen. I don't think she'd react that way. [Nancy, if you're reading this, I do/did/would not mean to hurt you in any way.]) The bible verse I'd like is Judges 4:21, because it might be ironic and lighten the mood, especially if she killed me in my sleep and/or with a stake.

I have an opening line for that, too. You could sort of shrug and say, "Well, Travis did marry Nancy for her *killer* body." (Nancy, if you are reading this, please stop.)

If Nancy and I aren't still together when I die, I'd like whatever girl I'm with to wear a black cocktail dress and one of those sexy hats Jackie Kennedy wore. Make sure Nancy gets invited. Disregard this if I die of some disease, because I'll have time to write up something more specific in the hospital. (Wearing a hazmat suit might be funny, like my body is contagious? Might not work if it's cancer.)

SAMUEL J. ADAMS was born in Tokyo and now lives in northern California, where he works with adults with disabilities. His stories appear, or are forthcoming, in *Ruminate*, *DIAGRAM*, *Moon City Review*, *Monkeybicycle*, *Atticus Review*, *Spork*, *New World Writing*, *Landlocked*, and elsewhere. He was recently a 2018 writing resident at Kimmel Harding Nelson Center for the Arts in Nebraska City, NE.

MICHAEL AGUGOM was born in Nigeria. He served as TV Presenter/ Reporter with the largest TV network in Africa. His fiction has been published in *Capra Review*, *Referential Magazine*, *Courtship of Wind*, *Hypertext Magazine*, and *Queer Africa 2: New Stories* (Ma Thoko's Books) and forthcoming in the *Cantabrigian Magazine*. He is a recipient of the Iceland Writers Retreat Alumni Award.

ZSOMBOR AURÉL BIRÓ was born in 1998 in Budapest, where he currently studies sociology at Eötvös Loránd University. His short stories have been published in a variety of prestigious Hungarian literary journals, including *Litera*, *Múút*, *Kortárs*, and *Szif Online*. "Sparrows" was originally published in the Hungarian anthology *Kóspallag 2018*.

TIMEA BALOGH is a Hungarian American writer and translator with an MFA in Fiction from the University of Nevada, Las Vegas. Her translations have appeared in *The Offing*, *The Short Story Project*, *Two Lines Journal*, *Arkansas International*, *elsewhere*, and *Wretched Strangers* an anthology by Boiler House Press. Her debut short story was published by *Juked* and was nominated for the PEN/Robert J. Dau Short Story Prize for Emerging Writers. She divides her time between Las Vegas and Budapest. You can tweet her at @TimeaRozalia.

RYAN W. BRADLEY has pumped gas, painted houses, swept the floor of a mechanic's shop, worked on a construction crew in the Arctic Circle, fronted a punk band, and more. He now works in marketing. He is the author of eight books, including *Nothing but the Dead and Dying*. He lives in Oregon with his wife and two sons.

ERICK BRUCKER is an essayist and fiction writer from Richmond, VA. His work has appeared or is forthcoming in *Jelly Bucket*, *Grasslimb*, and *BULL*. In hindsight, he misses working at Blockbuster and is planning a trip to Alaska so that he can wear his old uniform in the store one last time—he's convinced that this will offer him closure. He has an AAS in [General] from John Tyler Community College, a BA in Political Science from University of Richmond, and an MFA in Nonfiction Writing from University of Iowa.

ASHLEIGH BRYANT PHILLIPS is from Woodland, North Carolina. She wants to thank you for reading her work. Please read more at *Hobart*, *Tusk*, *Show Your Skin*, *drDoctor*, *People Holding*, *The Nervous Breakdown*, *Parhelion*, X-R-A-Y, and *Scalawag*.

LELAND CHEUK is the author of the story collection letters from *Dinosaurs* (2016) and the novel the *Misadventures of Sulliver Pong* (2015). His newest novel *No Good Very Bad Asian* is forthcoming from C&R press in 2019.

CHLOE N. CLARK's work has appeared in *Apex*, *Glass*, *Hobart*, *Little Fiction*, *Uncanny*, *Yes*, and more. She is co-EIC of *Cotton Xenomorph*, teaches at Iowa State University, and her debut chapbook *The Science of Unvanishing Objects* is out from Finishing Line Press and her full length collection, *Your Strange Fortune*, is due out from Vegetarian Alcoholic Press. Find her on Twitter @PintsNCupcakes

STEVE CHANG is from the San Gabriel Valley, California. He holds an MFA from Cornell University and is former bassist for Korean band GENIUS. His work has appeared or is forthcoming in *Guernica*, *Atticus Review*, *Jellyfish Review*, *North American Review*, and elsewhere. He likes reviews. He tweets at @steveXisXok.

CHRISTINA DALCHER makes things up and writes them down, occasionally from the point of view of a cat. She also made a book called *VOX*.

SCOTT DAUGHTRIDGE DEMER is a fiction writer from Atlanta, Georgia. His work has been featured in *Necessary Fiction*, *Midwestern Gothic*, *The Fanzine*, *Everyday Genius*, and other places. He currently studies writing at Arizona State University.

BRIAN ALAN ELLIS runs House of Vlad Press, and is the author of several books, including *Sad Laughter* (Civil Coping Mechanisms, 2018) and *Something to Do with Self-Hate* (House of Vlad/Talking Book, 2017). His writing has appeared at *Juked*, *Hobart*, *Monkeybicycle*, *Heavy Feather Review*, *Electric Literature*, *Vol. 1 Brooklyn*, *Fanzine*, *Queen Mob's Tea House*, and *Funhouse*. He lives in Florida.

MACK EISENMANN is a writer and occasional dancer living in North Dakota. Her fiction focuses on feminism and gender experience.

CADE carries the sole Y chromosome at home with his wife and two daughters. He lives in Las Vegas, where he is a managing editor of *Blue Draft Journal*. He's a hot-sauce connoisseur, a craft-beer enthusiast, and an ex-bodybuilder. His work has appeared in multiple journals, including *After the Pause* and *Typishly*.

Similar work by TIMSTON JOHNSTON can be found at *Cheap Pop*, *Denver Quarterly*, *Hobart* (online), and other admirable elsewheres. He is a pancake connoiSSEUR AND SOMETIMES ACCIDENTALLY HITS THE CAPS LOCK KEY.

ALICE KALTMAN is the author of the story collection *Staggerwing*, the novel *Wavehouse* and the forthcoming fantasy *The Tantalizing Tale Of Grace Minnaugh*. Her stories appear in numerous journals aside from the bodacious *BULL*, including *Hobart*, *Whiskey Paper*, *Joyland*, and in the anthologies *The Pleasure You Suffer* and *Feckless Cunt*. Her work has twice been selected as Longform Fiction Picks, and was selected as a semifinalist for The Best Small Fictions 2017. Alice lives, writes and surfs in Brooklyn and Montauk, New York

ELEANOR LEVINE's writing has appeared in more than 50 publications, including *Fiction*, *Evergreen Review*, *Fiction Southeast*, *Dos Passos Review*, *Hobart*, *Juked*, *The Denver Quarterly*, Pank, *The Toronto Quarterly*, *SRPR* (*Spoon River Poetry Review*), *Wigleaf*, *Heavy Feather Review*, *The Breakwater Review*, *Artemis*, *The Forward* and (*b*)*OINK*; forthcoming work in Willard & Maple. Levine's poetry collection, *Waitress at the Red Moon Pizzeria*, was released in 2016 by Unsolicited Press (Davis, California).

KIM MAGOWAN lives in San Francisco and teaches in the Department of Literatures and Languages at Mills College. Her short story collection *Undoing* won the 2017 Moon City Press Fiction Award and was published in March 2018. Her novel *The Light Source* is forthcoming from 7.13 Books in July 2019. Her fiction has been published in *Atticus Review, Bird's Thumb, Cleaver, The Gettysburg Review, Hobart, New World Writing, SmokeLong Quarterly*, and many other journals. She is Fiction Editor of *Pithead Chapel*.

DELVON T. MATTINGLY, who also goes by D.T. Mattingly, is an emerging fiction writer and a PhD student in epidemiology at the University of Michigan. His fiction has appeared in *Maudlin House, MoonPark Review*, and elsewhere. He currently lives in Ann Arbor, Michigan with his two cats, Liam and Tsuki. Learn more about his work at http://delvonmattingly.com. He tweets here: @delvonmattingly.

REBEKAH MORGAN lives in Appalachia. His writing has appeared at *Hobart, Anti-Heroin Chic, New York Tyrant, Bad Nudes, Instant, For Every Year, Faded Out, X-R-A-Y*, and *Witchcraft Magazine*.

HUN OHM Is a writer and intellectual property attorney. He lives in western Massachusetts. His fiction has appeared in *JMWW, Necessary Fiction, The Citron Review, Literary Orphans* and other publications.

PORTUGAL. THE MAN is a band. They play music. They write songs. The make coolassed videos. They say smart things in songs and interviews like this. You should check them out when you get done with this. Here's their web site: http://www.portugaltheman.com. They are cool.

FRANK REARDON was born in 1974 in Boston, Massachusetts, and currently lives in Minot, North Dakota. Frank has published poetry and short stories in many reviews, journals and online zines. His first poetry collection, *Interstate Chokehold*, was published by NeoPoiesis Press in 2009 as well as his second poetry collection *Nirvana Haymaker* in 2012. His third poetry collection *Blood Music* was published by Punk Hostage Press in 2013. In 2014 Reardon published a chapbook with Dog On A Chain Press titled *The Broken Halo Blues*. Frank is currently working on more short fiction.

ROB ROENSCH has an MFA from Cornell University. He is an Associate Professor in the English Department of Oklahoma City University and he lives in Oklahoma City with his wife and two daughters. He won the International Scott Prize for Short Stories in 2012 from Salt Publishing for his collection titled *The Wildflowers of Baltimore*. He was awarded the Peter Taylor Scholarship in Fiction to the 2018 Sewanee Writers' Conference.

T.L. SIMPSON is an award-winning sports journalist in Arkansas, where he lives and writes with his wife and three kids. He is currently at work on a novel. He can be found on Twitter @trvsimpson.

MISTY SKAGGS is an author, artist, activist and three time college drop out. She was born and raised in the backwoods of Eastern Kentucky, where she still resides out at the end of a gravel road in Elliott County. She currently serves as Appalachian Features Editor at *Rabble Lit*, a working class journal for the arts. Skaggs' roots show through in nearly every sentence and her poetry and prose have been featured in literary journals across the Appalachian region for well over a decade. When she isn't writing, the poet enjoys hitting up musty thrift stores, drinking too much coffee and growing a kickass garden. You can find more of her work online at rabblelit.com or at her blog, lipstickhick.tumblr.com.

BUD SMITH lives in Jersey City and works construction. He is the author of the novel *Teenager* (Tyrant Books '19), among others.

ADAM VAN WINKLE is the author of the novel, Abraham Anyhow, which was selected by Southern Literary Review as the June 2017 "Read of the Month." The follow up novel, While They were in the Field, releases in 2019. His prose has appeared in *Bull*, *Cheap POP!*, *Pithead Chapel*, *Steel Toe Review*, *Red Dirt Forum*, and elsewhere. A Pushcart nominee, Van Winkle is founder and editor-in-chief of *Cowboy Jamboree Magazine* and Press. Born and raised in Texoma on both sides of the Oklahoma-Texas border, he resides with his wife and animal pack on a rural route in Southern Illinois. Visit his website and Twitter handle at www.adamvanwinkle.com and @gritvanwinkle.

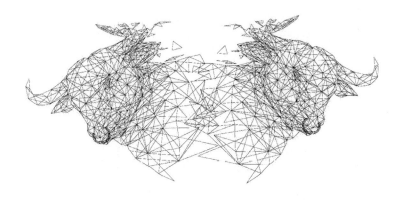